"Hello, *Amber,*" Marco said, with dark, steely mockery in his tone.

"What are you doing here?" she gasped, her heart contracting into a shriveled ball. "How did you find me?"

His expression changed slightly, as if she'd just satisfied him in some way. "We must talk."

He took her arm but she shook off his hand. "I don't need to talk to you," she said, trying to sidestep him. But this time he caught her arm in an unshakable grip, trying to walk her along with him.

"Come—we cannot discuss anything here."

"I'm not going anywhere with you. Let go of me or I'll scream." She opened her mouth and he dropped his hand from her arm, looking grimly amused.

"And I will tell people you are attempting to deprive me of my legal rights by fraud and deception. I wish to talk about your sister."

Her *sister?* Of course—he'd called her by her own name, which she'd automatically reacted to. Not Azure's. How much did he know? "How did you find out where I work?"

"I hired an investigator," he said calmly.

"You...?" For a second she was stunned as well as angry. The idea of a stranger prying into her life gave her the creeps. "How dare you!"

"How else could I discover the truth? You lied to me."

DAPHNE CLAIR lives in subtropical New Zealand with her Dutch-born husband. They have five children. At eight years old she embarked on her first novel, about taming a tiger. This epic never reached a publisher, but metamorphosed male tigers still prowl the pages of her romances, of which she has written more than thirty for Harlequin and more than sixty all told. Her other writing includes nonfiction, poetry and short stories, and she has won literary prizes in New Zealand and America.

Readers are invited to visit Daphne Clair's Web site at www.daphneclair.com.

SALZANO'S CAPTIVE BRIDE

DAPHNE CLAIR

~ FORCED TO MARRY ~

HARLEQUIN®

TORONTO • NEW YORK • LONDON
AMSTERDAM • PARIS • SYDNEY • HAMBURG
STOCKHOLM • ATHENS • TOKYO • MILAN • MADRID
PRAGUE • WARSAW • BUDAPEST • AUCKLAND

Recycling programs for this product may not exist in your area.

ISBN-13: 978-0-373-52726-7

SALZANO'S CAPTIVE BRIDE

First North American Publication 2009.

Copyright © 2009 by Daphne Clair.

www.eHarlequin.com

Printed in U.S.A.

SALZANO'S
CAPTIVE BRIDE

CHAPTER ONE

AMBER Odell had just washed up after her solitary evening meal when the doorbell sounded a long, imperative ring.

She closed a cupboard door with a click of the old-fashioned catch, hastily hung the tea towel on its rail and hurried along the short hallway.

The rimu floorboards beneath the faded carpet runner creaked under her bare feet. The old building in a once-fashionable Auckland suburb had endured a chequered career from grand home to orphanage to boarding house until, towards the end of the twentieth century, some crude renovations had converted it into flats. Amber was lucky to have leased one on the ground floor at a reasonable price, in return for some badly needed redecorating.

She switched on the porch light and hesitated at the sight of a large, dark shape behind the blue-and-red stained glass panes on the top part of the door. After a second or two the shape moved and raised a hand to rap on the wooden panel between the panes.

Cautiously she opened the door, braced to slam it shut again.

The porch light shone down on glossy waves of night-black hair combed back from an arresting olive-toned face with high cheekbones and a commanding nose. The forbidding features and uncompromising, beard-shadowed jaw were at odds with a sensuous male mouth, even though at the moment it was stubbornly set and unsmiling.

Vaguely she was conscious of broad shoulders, a pristine white T-shirt moulded over a toned chest, and long powerful legs encased in olive-green trousers. Casual clothes that somehow managed to convey a sense of style and expense.

But most of her attention was riveted by a nearly coal-dark gaze, burning with what looked like anger.

Which didn't make sense. She'd never laid eyes on the man in her life.

Not that he wasn't worth laying eyes on. She was perturbed by a stirring of unbidden female response to the potent aura of masculinity that invisibly cloaked him.

Pushing back a strand of fine, fair hair that flowed over shoulders bared by her brief tube top, she opened her mouth to ask what he wanted.

Before she could say anything, a comprehensive, searing gaze traversed downward over the wide strip of ribbed cotton hugging her breasts, and lingered on the pale flesh between the top and her blue shorts before quickly taking in the length of her legs and then returning to her face.

Amber went hot all over with anger of her own—and shock at the way her pulse points had leapt to life under the bold inspection. Lifting her chin—as she needed to anyway to look the man in the eye—she was about to ask again what he wanted when he forestalled her with the abrupt query "Where is he?" issued in a low, grating voice.

She blinked, startled. "I think you've—" *Made a mistake,* she'd been going to say, but she was cut off.

"I said, *Where is he?*" the man rasped. "Where is my son?"

"Well, certainly not here!" Amber told him. Maybe he was looking for one of the other tenants. "You've got the wrong place. Sorry."

She began to close the door, but the man reached out and with apparent ease pushed it back again and stepped into the hallway.

Amber instinctively retreated, then realised that was the worst thing to do as the intimidating stranger kicked the door shut behind him, and when she turned to flee along the passageway—not that it would do her much good—a hard hand clamped about her arm and swung her to face him.

She opened her mouth to scream, hoping the two students next door or the journalist in the flat directly above hers would hear and investigate.

All she got out was a choked sound before the intruder put his other hand over her mouth and crowded her against the wall. She felt the warmth of his lean, hard body almost touching hers, and smelled a faint whiff of leather with a hint of newly cut grass. Aftershave? Although he looked as if he hadn't shaved for a couple of days.

He said, moderating his voice with its slight foreign accent in an apparent effort to reassure her, "Don't be foolish. You have no need to fear me."

Now he looked exasperated rather than angry. Amber contemplated kneeing him, weighing her chances of disabling him and escaping, but suddenly he let her go and said, "Now let us be sensible."

Yes, let's! Amber thought grimly. "The sensible thing is for you to leave before I call the police!"

A frown appeared between his dark brows, and a flash of temper lit his eyes again. He said flatly, "All I ask is to see my son. You have—"

"I told you—" Amber raised her voice "—your son is not here! I don't know why you should think—"

"I don't believe you."

"Look—" she edged towards the door and kept talking "—you've made a mistake. I can't help you, and I'm asking you to leave."

"Leave?" He seemed affronted. "After flying from Venezuela to New Zealand? I have not slept since—"

"That's not my problem," she informed him.

She reached out to open the door again but he put a hand on it, holding it shut and looking down at her through narrowed eyes. "If he is not here," he said quietly, as though struggling to control himself, "what have you done with him?"

A new expression had appeared in his eyes—surely not fear? Or at least genuine anxiety.

"Nothing!"

Again the black brows drew together. Lucifer must have had that same terrible, ferocious male beauty.

She shivered, and he said, the harsh note back in his voice, "What are you up to?" His eyes made another hostile survey of her. "If you ever had a child it certainly does not show."

Amber gaped. "I've never had a child!" She reminded herself that most mentally ill people weren't dangerous.

Then he grabbed her upper arms and she thought, *But a few are!* and forced herself not to kick and hit. That might trigger him into real violence. If she kept calm maybe she could talk him into leaving. He muttered something that sounded suspiciously like swearing in Spanish. White teeth showed as his lips curled back in a near-snarl. "What devil's game are you playing?" he demanded. "Why did you write to me?"

"*Write* to you?" Amber's voice rose in disbelief. "I don't even *know* you!"

His hands tightened until she winced, and he dropped them, his tawny skin darkening. "In a sense that is true," he said with an air of hauteur, his eyes almost hidden by lowered lids that had the longest, thickest lashes she'd ever seen on a man. "But for a short time we *knew* each other intimately. That you cannot deny."

About to do so in no uncertain terms, she hesitated as a fantastic suspicion slithered into her mind. *Venezuela.* South America.

No. She shook her head to dislodge the shameful notion. The guy was raving.

"Very well," he said, impatient again and misinterpreting her action. "It is a matter of semantics. It was not… an emotional intimacy. But whatever you call it, you have not forgotten. What did you expect when you wrote that letter? That I would send money and put it out of my mind?"

"Wh-which letter?" Was it possible…? *No!*

"Were there others?" he asked, the lift of those almost satanic brows expressing cynical doubt. "The one," he continued with exaggerated patience, "that asked for a *contribution* towards the welfare of the child you had borne, apparently to me."

For a moment Amber felt dizzy, sick, and her hand involuntarily flew to her mouth to stop an exclamation escaping. Her voice shaking, she said, "I never sent you any letter, I swear."

Maybe she'd got through to him at last. He appeared briefly disconcerted, then his expression hardened again. "You were desperate, it said. Was it simply an attempt at extortion and there truly is no child?"

She breathed in, thinking, and slowly said, "Would you believe me if I told you that you have the wrong woman?"

His brows shot up again and he laughed. Not pleasantly. "I know I had far more wine that night than was wise, but I was not so drunk that I don't remember the face of the woman I shared a bed with."

Feeling sicker still, her heart pounding erratically, Amber couldn't speak.

Not that she'd have had a chance. His lips curling in a sneer, he asked, "Do you make a habit of asking men to pay you off after…I believe you would call it a one-night stand."

"I don't do one-night stands," she flashed, "and neither—" caution intervened "—neither do I try to blackmail…anybody."

"I'm the only one so privileged?" he asked, the harsh, accusative tone turning dark and silken, which paradoxically made her feel even more threatened. "And if it was not a one-night stand I'm not sure what you think it was. You yourself have denied any real connection between us, and we have had no contact since—until you claimed to have borne me a son."

"I haven't claimed anything of the sort!" Amber snapped. And as he made a move towards her, fright and anger sharpened her voice. "Don't you dare come near me!"

He stopped dead, as if she'd shot him. "I will not hurt you," he said.

"Oh, really?" She hoped her derisive tone didn't set him off, but she couldn't help adding acidly, "I expect I'll have bruises on my arms tomorrow."

To her surprise, a look of chagrin crossed his face. Stiffly, his accent stronger, he said, "If that is so, I apologise. I was…not thinking."

Not hard to guess he wasn't accustomed to apologising.

The change in him was at least marginally reassuring. Encouraged, Amber tried again, even more forcefully. "You're not listening to me, are you? I don't *know*—"

"Why should I listen to lies?"

"I'm not lying. You've got it all wrong!"

The sound he made in his throat was akin to an animal growl, alarming her again. He reached out, and long fingers closed about her wrist. "Then show me he is not here."

She wanted to snap at him again, but perhaps it would be safer to humour the man, persuade him he'd made a mistake, and he might leave. Or to distract him so she'd have a shot at escaping. "All right," she said finally. It wouldn't take long—the flat had only three small rooms besides the kitchen and bathroom. "Feel free to look around."

His gaze suspicious, he tugged at her imprisoned wrist. "Show me."

She wasn't going to be given a chance to flee outside and call for help.

Amber shrugged, hiding the fact that her heart was thumping, and led him to the doorway of her cosy sitting room, reaching aside to switch on the light.

A soft, cushioned olive-green sofa faced the fireplace, in front of which she'd placed a Chinese jar filled with white plumes of native toe-toe.

Two armchairs with calico slip-covers hiding their shabby upholstery were set at right-angles to the sofa, a couple of bright-red wooden boxes serving as end tables. Her TV and sound system sat in the chimney corners, and on the mantel a row of books was held by the South Island jade bookends she'd inherited from her grandmother.

The man glanced over the room without entering, and Amber took him across the hallway to her bedroom.

The bed was covered in white *broderie-anglaise,* and

thick sheepskin rugs lay on the varnished floor. This time the man walked into the room as she tugged her wrist from his grip and stepped to one side, leaning with folded arms against the curve of the second-hand Queen Anne style dressing table.

The man threw her a glance that gave a silent warning and strode to the mirror-doored wardrobe, briefly looked at the clothes hanging there and closed it again. When his gaze went to the dressing table drawers she looked back at him defiantly and said, "You are *not* going through my underwear drawers. Are you some kind of pervert?"

For an instant fury flared in his eyes, then she thought he almost laughed, and she could see he was weighing whether he should ignore her ban before he headed for the door. Amber breathed a little more easily.

"Sure you don't want to look under the bed?" she inquired as he snagged her wrist again.

He didn't respond to the sarcasm, merely striding down the hall to the door opening into the minuscule bathroom.

Obviously no one was lurking in the shower cubicle behind its clear plastic curtain printed with coloured fish, or hiding in the cupboard beneath the washbasin.

Next was her office-cum-spare room, hardly large enough for the single guest bed, her filing cabinet, a compact desk that held her laptop computer, and the crowded shelves of reference books along one wall.

That left the narrow kitchen with a small dining area at one end. The man opened the back door onto the little walled and paved patio, saw the potted plants and the wrought-iron table and chairs for two, and on closing the door allowed her to free herself of his grasp and retreat against the sink counter.

He turned to the bank of cupboards on the opposite

wall, and the counter below that held her toaster and bread-bin. Amber noticed how the glossy black hair was allowed to flow past his nape and curl at the neckline of his T-shirt.

Wondering if she could make a dash along the passage-way to the front door, she saw his shoulders stiffen, his entire body go utterly still. Had he stopped breathing?

He reached for something, making a hissing sound between his teeth, and turned abruptly to face her. "If you have no child, what is this?"

Oh, Lord! she prayed, staring at the baby's pacifier in his broad palm. *How do I get out of this?* "My...my friend must have left it when she brought her baby to visit."

His hand closed over the small object, then he dropped it onto the counter and began opening cupboard doors, shifting jars and bottles and tins, cups and plates, until in a lower cupboard he found a basket filled with small stuffed toys, a board book, rattles, a toy xylophone and a jumble of plastic blocks.

"For visiting children," she said. "Some of my friends have babies or toddlers. You won't find anything else. I keep telling you, you've made a mistake!"

He whirled then, fixing her with a glittering, hostile stare. "My mistake was almost two years ago, when I was *estúpido* enough to let cheap wine and a pretty tourist send my good sense and *disciplina* to the winds."

Bristling at his dismissal of the "pretty tourist" as on a par with "cheap wine," Amber said, "Whatever your problem is—"

"It is *our* problem," he argued, "if what was in that letter is true. No matter how often you deny it, or how distaste-ful I find it."

Distasteful? If that was how he thought of his supposed offspring, what sort of a father would he be?

The thought validated her caution. "Look," she said, making her denial as authoritative as she could, "it wasn't me. And I don't feel well." Brushing another strand of hair from her cheek, she realised her hand was trembling. Her stomach was battling nausea and her knees felt watery.

His eyes searched her face with patent distrust. "You are pale," he allowed grudgingly. His mouth clamped for a moment before he said, "Tomorrow then. I will come back. And I warn you, if you are not here I will find you again."

"How *did* you…?" Curious as to how he'd landed on *her* doorstep, she paused to reword the question. "You can't have had *my* address." She'd been too confused and alarmed to think about that.

A hint of that menacing sneer again distorted the firm male mouth. "It was not difficult. The post office box given as the return address was in Auckland, New Zealand. And you are the only A. Odell in the telephone book."

"I don't have a box," she said. "And not everyone is in the phone book." Which was lucky for them. It kept scary foreign men from pushing uninvited into their homes and flinging wild accusations.

She put a hand on the counter behind her. Her legs were still unsteady, and her voice lacked any kind of confidence when she said, "Please would you leave now? I…really can't talk to you any more tonight."

He took a step towards her, the Lucifer frown reappearing. "Are you ill? Do you need help?" One hand moved as if to touch her, but she shrank from it.

"All I need is for you to go!" And now she sounded shrill, dammit.

To her infinite relief he nodded curtly, but said, "You will be here tomorrow." As if he could order it. "In the morning?"

He was trying to pin her down. "I have to work," she

said. "Some people do, you know." While some could afford to fly across the world at the drop of a hat—or a letter. "Tomorrow evening," she suggested randomly. "Eight o'clock." It seemed the only way to get rid of him, and next time she'd make sure she wasn't alone.

Another nod, and he turned to leave. Amber heard his footsteps recede down the passageway, and the door closing. Slumping against the counter, she felt as if she'd been picked up by a hurricane and dropped back to earth.

She straightened and made herself a cup of hot, black coffee, added a generous spoonful of sugar and took it to her bedroom. Sitting on the bed, she downed several steadying sips, before picking up the phone and keying in a number.

The ringing went on for a long time, but she didn't hang up. When it finally stopped and a voice as familiar as her own answered, she said without preamble, "Azzie, what on *earth* have you done?"

CHAPTER TWO

MARCO Enrique Salvatore Costa Salzano wasn't accustomed to being brushed off by women, much less being evicted from their homes.

But neither was he in the habit of forcibly invading those homes.

He'd spent the day brooding over last night's debacle even while he made a time-killing exploration of Auckland city and its environs, ending with a stroll on the waterfront path that curved in and out along several bays overlooked by well-kept houses wherever steep cliffs didn't border the road.

He'd found an underwater aquarium that featured such sea creatures as huge stingrays and even medium-size sharks swimming freely behind glass above and around the visitors. A short trolley ride in a fake Antarctic section allowed them to come eye to eye with king penguins. The animals were in every way a world apart from those he was accustomed to and to which he devoted a large part of his time. Yet they were sufficiently fascinating that for a short while he'd almost forgotten the mission that had brought him to the South Pacific.

Now the sun was inching downward and the eye-watering blue of the sky over the Waitemata Harbour had gradually softened to a paler shade while he paced the thick carpet of his hotel suite. The hands of his watch crawled towards seven-thirty so slowly that he wondered if the several thousand dollars he'd paid for its world-renowned brand reliability, expensive platinum casing and flawless design had been misspent. There was still more than half an hour to his appointment with the woman who last night had inexplicably denied knowing him.

When he'd finally arrived in New Zealand after a seemingly endless flight, perhaps he shouldn't have left the hotel as soon as he'd had a hurried shower and pulled clean clothes randomly from his bag. Jet-lagged though he was, he hadn't been able to tolerate another night of angry anticipation mingled with regret and self-castigation—and something he refused to name as confused hope.

After all that, and despite her having appealed for his help in a way that suggested she and *his son* were suffering imminent if not actual penury, the woman had tried to shut the door on him!

Unable to conceal his simmering rage, he knew he had made her nervous. Although she'd mounted a valiant effort to hide that, standing up to him and threatening to call the police.

He almost smiled, recalling the defiant flash of her eyes—he hadn't remembered she had such striking eyes, truly jade green ringed with amber—and her determined efforts to oust him from that matchbox of a home. She'd deliberately goaded him with sarcasm and insults despite her slight though very feminine build and the fact that the top of her head barely reached his chin.

When he'd silenced her attempt to scream, and blocked her escape with his body, her hair had been soft and silky against his throat and smelled of apricots with a hint of fresh lemon.

That scent had unexpectedly aroused him, as had the tantalising way her breasts rose and fell with her frightened breathing, under the scanty piece of cloth that barely covered them. He'd quickly stepped back, not wanting to add fear of rape to her perplexing reactions. It was not in his nature to terrorise women.

Admittedly last night's confrontation had been no ordinary visit. Perhaps he could have been less impetuous, but that letter had been a bombshell, coming long after he had written off the *Carnaval* incident as a lapse in judgement that, fortunately, had had no serious consequences.

Why be afraid of a man she'd happily allowed to take her to an unknown destination in a foreign city to have sex when they'd only met a couple of hours before? And why deny she'd sent that letter? Any logical reason eluded him.

Unless the story had been a lie. His fists clenched and he stopped pacing to stare moodily at the harbour, now calming into a tranquil satin expanse at odds with his chaotic thoughts. If this whole thing was a fabrication, he'd wasted his time making a long, time-consuming journey at great inconvenience to himself, his business and his family.

And the woman he'd done it for deserved no respect and no consideration.

Her apartment was old and the rooms cramped, her furnishings simple, but he'd seen no sign of true poverty. He wondered if New Zealanders knew the meaning of the word.

No one was dressed in rags, and although occasional buskers performed, and a few street sellers displayed cheap jewellery or carvings, no whining beggars or persistent thin-faced children had accosted him.

Again he consulted his watch, seemingly for the hun-

dredth time in the last hour, then left his room and took the
elevator to the main entrance, where the doorman hailed
him a taxi.

A couple of minutes before eight Amber's doorbell rang
in the same imperious way it had the previous night.

All day her nerves had been strung to screaming point.

She loved her job as a researcher for a film and TV pro-
duction company and usually gave it her all, but today her
mind had kept straying to an exotic-looking, disturbing and
driven male who would be on her doorstep again that night.
During a team meeting she'd realised she hadn't heard a
word for the past five or ten minutes, and the end of her
ballpoint pen showed teeth marks where she'd been
absently chewing on it.

And Azzie had been totally immovable about joining
her tonight, leaving Amber to deal with the formidable
Venezuelan on her own.

At the sound of the doorbell, she finished tying the
white-and-green wraparound skirt that she'd teamed with
a sleeveless white lawn top fastened with tiny pearl buttons.
She slipped her feet into wedge-heeled casual shoes that
gave her a few extra inches, and hastily pinned her hair into
a knot while walking to the door.

The man who stood there was as striking as she remembered, but now he wore dark trousers, a cream shirt open
at the collar, and a light, flecked cream jacket. The barely
contained fury of last night had abated. He looked rigidly
contained and rather chilly when she stepped back and
said, "Come in, *señor.*"

His black brows lifted a fraction as he stepped into the
hallway. "So formal," he said, "after having my baby?"

Amber bit her lip. "We…we can't talk here." She gestured

towards the living room and he nodded, then placed a hand lightly on her waist, guiding her into the room ahead of him. A startling quiver of sexual awareness made her move quickly away from him to one of the armchairs, but she remained standing. Trying to match his self-possession, she offered, "Can I get you a coffee or something?"

"I did not come here for coffee. Please sit down."

Not expressing her resentment at being told to sit down in her own living room, she perched on the edge of one of the armchairs and waited while he took the opposite one.

Figuring that getting in first was the best plan of attack, Amber broke into speech. "I'm sorry you came all this way for nothing, but that letter was a mistake. I—"

"So you admit writing it?"

"It should never have been sent," she said, choosing her words as if picking her way through a minefield. "I'm sorry if it misled you."

His lips tightened, and for a moment she thought she saw disappointment in his eyes. "Misled me?" he said, and now she could see nothing in the dark depths but condemnation.

Her fingers clasped tightly together against a childish urge to cross them behind her back, she said, "The letter didn't say the baby was yours. Did it?" she added, trying to sound authoritative.

"The implication—" he started to say before she hurried on.

"I'm sorry if it wasn't clear, but it was written in haste and…and a silly panic. You had said in Caracas—" she paused to ensure she was quoting exactly "—'If you have any problem, contact me.'" Despite herself she felt her cheeks growing hot. Would he recall exactly how he had couched the offer?

A flash of incredulity crossed his controlled features.

Amber ploughed ahead. "The letter was just a stupid impulse. It wasn't necessary for you to come all this way. That was quite—" disastrous "—unexpected. So you can go home and forget about it. I'm sorry," she repeated under his hostile stare.

He stood up so suddenly she jumped, and stiffened her spine to stop herself shrinking from him.

Even though he didn't come nearer, his stance and the renewed anger in his blazing eyes, the stern line of his mouth, made her heart do a somersault. "Go?" he said. "Just so?" He snapped his fingers and again Amber flinched.

"I know you've come a long way," she said placatingly, "and I'm really sor—"

"Do not tell me again that you are *sorry!*" he snarled. "You claimed to have given birth to a baby boy nine months after we…met in Caracas. What was I supposed to think? And what did *you* think? That I'm the kind of man who would pay off the mother of my child and then wash my hands of them both?"

Amber swallowed hard. "I don't know what kind of man you are," she admitted. "Except that you're…" wealthy, aristocratic, and apparently some kind of power in his own country. Besides having a temper.

"That I have money?" he finished for her scornfully. "And you thought you could milk me of some of that money without giving anything in return. Was that why this letter promised never to bother me again?"

"It wasn't like that!"

He surged forward, gripping the arms of her chair, and now she instinctively drew back. "If there ever was such a child," he said, not loudly but in an implacable voice that sent a shiver down her spine, "where is he?"

Unable to meet his accusing eyes, she stared down at her entwined hands. "As I said last night, I've never had a baby." Despite doing what she'd been convinced was the right thing, she had a ghastly sense of wrongness.

"You wrote that you had debts you were unable to pay, that you were on the point of losing your home. It seemed my son was being thrown onto the street."

"Um," she muttered. "It wasn't as bad as that, exactly. Things are improving now."

"How? You found some other poor fool to fall for your tricks?" He lifted one hand from the chair arm, only to grasp her chin and make her look up at him.

"No!" she said. "Nothing of the sort."

His eyes, filled with accusation, were inches away. "The problem with liars," he said, "is that one never knows when they are telling the truth."

She forced herself to look straight into those dark eyes. "I did not have your baby. And I'm not lying." *I'm not,* she assured herself. "You saw last night there's no baby here."

He scrutinised her for what seemed like minutes. Then abruptly he released her chin and straightened, stepping back but still watching her with patent mistrust. "Are you a gambler?" he asked.

"What?" She didn't understand the switch of subject.

"Was that why you needed money?"

She shook her head. "It isn't important now."

"You have put me to a great deal of trouble and some expense. I think I have a right to ask why."

"I'm sor—" He lifted a warning hand and she stopped the apology leaving her tongue. She said instead, "If you want your airfare reimbursed…" It seemed only fair to offer.

The twist of his lips was hardly a smile, although he

seemed to derive some kind of sardonic amusement from her reply. He made a dismissive gesture. "That is not necessary, even if it is possible."

She had been rash to suggest it. He'd probably travelled first class, and after paying off the student loan that had got her through university with degrees in history and media studies, and finally being able to afford her own place instead of grungy shared digs, her savings were on the lean side of modest. As for Azzie—no use even thinking about it.

Growing bolder, she stood up, still finding him much too close. Her knees were watery. "Thank you. I think you'd better go now. There's nothing more I can tell you."

"You mean there is nothing more you wish to tell me."

Amber shrugged. What else could she say without arousing further suspicion? And she needed him to leave. Marco Salzano's presence was unnerving in more than one way. While his scorn and disbelief were intimidating, he was a powerfully attractive man, and her female hormones ran riot every time he came near. She was beginning to have a new understanding of what had taken place in Venezuela.

Marco turned and took a couple of steps away from her. She inwardly sighed in relief, but then he stopped and faced her again. His gaze sharpened and he tilted his head. "Why," he said slowly, "have I a…a sense that you are hiding something? Perhaps something I should know?"

Her mouth dried and she said in a near-whisper, "There is no reason to involve you in my troubles."

As if on impulse he plunged a hand into an inside pocket of his jacket, took out a leather wallet and pulled a bundle of notes from it.

They were New Zealand notes. Reddish, hundred-dollar

ones. Amounting to more money than Amber had ever seen anyone handle so casually.

"Take it," he said, holding the cash out to her, his expression unreadable. "Let us say for remembrance of a pleasurable encounter."

Amber recoiled. "I can't take your money!"

A gleam of surprised speculation lit his eyes and she knew she'd made a mistake. "But that is exactly why I am here," he said softly, "is it not?"

"I told you, everything's all right now." She fervently hoped so. Her hands were clasped behind her back, her mouth set in stubborn refusal.

He studied her as if she were a puzzle he had trouble figuring out, even while he tucked the notes back into the wallet and returned it to his pocket. Unnerved by the scrutiny, Amber lifted a hand to brush back a wayward strand of hair that was tickling the corner of her mouth.

His eyes tracked the movement, and when she made to lower her hand he suddenly covered the space between them in a stride, catching her forearm near the elbow so that it remained raised while he inspected the inside of her upper arm. Following his gaze, she saw a thumb-shaped bruise marring the tender skin.

Her cheeks warmed and she tried to pull away, but he retained his firm though careful hold. She saw him take a breath, and his mouth compressed. She guessed he was keeping back some vivid language.

In a low voice she'd not heard from him before, he said, "Is that my mark?" He was still looking at the bruise, as if unwilling to meet her eyes. The moment lengthened unbearably. She could smell again that subtle leather-and-grass aroma, mingled with a combination of male skin scent and freshly laundered clothing.

"It doesn't matter," she said.

Totally unexpectedly the dark head bent and she felt his lips touch the blue mark.

She almost choked on an indrawn breath, biting her lip fiercely to stop an involuntary sound escaping from her throat, where her heart seemed to have lodged.

His hair swept against her skin, and the sensation was like a lightning bolt arrowing through her body.

What *was* that? Did Marco Salzano's surprisingly soft hair hold an electrical charge like the one that made her own hair crackle sometimes when she brushed it?

He lifted his head and the glitter in his eyes made her pulse roar into overdrive.

Slowly he lowered her arm, slipping his hand like a caress down to her wrist. "Such delicate skin," he murmured. "Forgive me."

Unable to speak for the rioting of her senses, Amber dazedly wondered how a mere fleeting touch could arouse such an extravagance of feeling. No one had the right to effortlessly exude that much sex appeal.

He seemed a tad bemused himself. His jaw went tight, and the taut skin over his cheekbones darkened further.

Gathering her wits from wherever they'd dispersed themselves, Amber pulled at her imprisoned wrist, and with apparent reluctance he released it, thrusting his hand into the pocket of his trousers.

"I did not remember what a desirable woman you are," he said. "It is not so surprising I lost my head that night, and stepped outside the bounds of my normal behaviour."

Had he? "You weren't the only one," she told him dryly. And then warned herself, *Shut up!*

He looked at her consideringly. "The woman I took to my bed in Caracas was no spotless virgin, I think."

Amber snapped, "That doesn't make her a slut!" Momentarily she closed her eyes. Had she blown it with that automatic defence?

Apparently unperturbed, he said, "I did not mean to imply such a thing. Merely that I assumed you were a woman of the world. Capable of protecting yourself from any…inconvenience. You yourself assured me of that afterwards, if you remember."

That jolted her. "I…don't remember," she claimed truthfully, hoping to close the subject. "Now would you—"

' "Had you had so much to drink?" he queried, frowning again. "I don't knowingly take advantage of drunken women. You appeared well aware of what you were doing. And I believe from your reactions at the time that you very much enjoyed our…brief encounter. You remember *that?*" The gleam that had entered his eyes intensified, and his mouth curved a little at the corners.

Heat rose again to Amber's cheeks. Desperately she said, "No. Now—"

"No?" Faint annoyance showed for an instant, and she supposed she'd offended his machismo.

The way he let his gaze roam over her body didn't help her flush subside. "Perhaps," he said in a reflective tone like a tiger's purr, "I can refresh your memory."

The sound she made when he swiftly closed the space between them again was something between a gasp and a squeal, but before she could say anything coherent he had his arms around her and had pulled her close, her body arching against the solid masculine warmth of his. Even as she opened her mouth to protest he covered it with his own, tipping her head back, his breath mingling with hers.

His lips were gentle but questing, moving across her startled ones even after she raised her hands to push at him.

The tip of his tongue was tracing an erotic path along her upper lip, igniting a shocking flare of answering desire before she rallied enough to clench her hands into fists and shove them against his chest.

His hands fell, and Amber shakily stepped back.

A glittering gaze met hers, and she swallowed before saying in a voice unlike her own, "I want you out of here right *now*."

As if he hadn't heard, he said, "I also seem to have forgotten much." She didn't know whether to be pleased or alarmed that he looked nearly as stunned as she felt. "You taste of honey…and passion," he said. "Something else I failed to remember."

He probably remembered nothing but wine, but she didn't want to go into that. Nor did she want to fall under the spell he'd woven with that oh-so-sexy, devastating kiss. "I said I want you to go," she stated precisely. "Please."

His expression became baffled, but he gave a jerky little bow of his head and said, "If you truly wish it."

"Yes." Not trusting herself to say more, she marched past him to the hallway and flung the front door open. "Our business is finished," she said as he passed her.

He turned then, a half-amused, half-rueful smile on his lips, his eyes making another leisurely, perhaps slightly perplexed examination of her entire body before he gave a brief shake of his head, then descended the shallow steps and strode away.

Tempted to yell a rude word or two after him, she resisted and instead closed the door with a snap and leaned back against it until her legs regained some strength.

Never in her life had she imagined being caught in a trap like this.

One day she'd stop feeling so damned guilty, because wasn't it all for the best?

Of course, she assured herself. For him as well as for…well, everyone.

She hadn't said anything that wasn't true.

A flimsy excuse. But she ought to be happy at emerging unscathed and just forget the whole thing ever happened.

Forget?

She lifted the back of her hand to scrub at her lips, which still tingled with the memory of Marco Salzano's kiss.

CHAPTER THREE

THE following day, instead of driving home after work, Amber took the route to her sister's home.

The seventies house that Azure and her husband, Rickie, were gradually restoring with Amber's occasional help was in an outer suburb where real estate was less horrendously expensive than in more fashionable areas.

Sitting at the scarred auction-bargain table in the big kitchen, Amber sipped at the cheap wine her sister had poured. Azure was on her second glass, and was now smiling at the plump, rosy-cheeked baby on her knee—a smile so special it caught at Amber's heart—but the baby, unimpressed, wrinkled his face up and whimpered crossly.

Azure handed him over to his aunt while she poured milk into a plastic sippy cup.

Amber bent to kiss the amazingly smooth, warm skin of the baby's temple and studied him while he looked at her interestedly with round eyes so dark she couldn't determine their colour, and he babbled in his own private language interspersed with the odd Mama and Dada and even Namba which Amber hoped was his effort at Auntie Amber.

Rickie's eyes were dark too, inherited from his Maori grandfather along with the black curls that Benny's soft fuzz promised to duplicate.

In the baby's blob of a nose, chubby face and tiny pouting little mouth there was certainly no hint of the man who had filled Amber's flat with his utterly adult male presence and striking features.

Seeing his mother approach with the cup, the little boy wriggled to the floor with a demanding "Ma!"

"At the table," she said firmly, perching him again on her own knee as she sat down.

"Azure," Amber felt driven to say, "you're sure there's no chance he's Mr. Salzano's baby?"

She recognised with a sinking feeling a flicker of fear in her sister's guileless eyes, belying Azure's defiant, "I told you, he misunderstood my letter. I never said that!"

"But you did have sex with him." Unbelievable though it seemed, Azure had confessed to that when Amber pressed her about the mysterious Venezuelan.

"*Once.* Oh, don't remind me!" Azure wailed. Benny stopped drinking his milk and began to wail too.

She soothed him, and when he settled again she said, "I didn't stop taking the pill until after that night. Once Rickie and I had decided we'd get married when we came home it didn't seem important. And I've never slept with anyone but Rickie before or since. So it can't be—"

"You did use a condom that night?" Something she'd assumed when she'd cornered her sister the day previously.

Azure shrugged. "What does it matter?" she muttered, her eyes fixed on the baby.

Amber was horrified. "You took an awful risk with a stranger!"

"We weren't thinking. Too much wine, I guess. He was mortified when he realised… It's okay, I had all kinds of tests when I found out I was pregnant. I don't want to talk about it any more, now Benny's safe. You didn't tell Marco about him, did you? You promised!"

Amber *had* promised in the end despite huge reluctance, faced with an hysterical but persuasive sister whose reasoning seemed fireproof, and who fervently swore there was no way her baby's father could be anyone other than the man who was now her husband. "No. But if there's any chance Benny's his—"

"Everyone says Benny looks like his dad. *You* did!"

Amber had, before a dark-haired, dark-eyed man appeared on her doorstep with a fantastic accusation that Azure had later convinced her wasn't possible.

Amber closed her eyes—a mistake. The shadowy figure lurking in the back of her mind became a full-blown living-colour picture of a tall, gorgeous man with a blaze of anger in his almost-black eyes and a mouth that, despite its seductive contours, expressed an unbending will when it wasn't twisted in contemptuous disbelief.

A mouth that could also be gentle, persuasive, despite his suspicion of her and his angry frustration—a mouth that had wrought some kind of erotic magic on her senses.

And though his eyes had blazed in fury, they had shown unwilling but genuine concern when he'd seen she felt ill.

Opening her own eyes, she demanded, "*Why* ask Marco Salzano for money, then?"

"Like I said before," Azure retorted, "money's nothing to people like him. His family made a fortune mining gold and diamonds way back—and later, oil."

"He told you that?" Boastful on top of everything.

"Sort of. He was so casual about it I knew he wasn't having me on. And I picked up some information later about the family. They're big landowners, well-known and still seriously rich. You should have seen the place he took me to." Awe momentarily lit Azure's eyes, then she blushed. "And that was just his city pad."

No sleazy by-the-hour hotel, then. Of course not, for a man with his innate male elegance and what her and Azure's grandmother would call breeding, undiminished by the rough beard shadow and his cavalier attitude towards Amber. He had, after all, mistaken her for her sister.

Despite the three years' difference in their ages, people often mistook one of the Odell girls for the other.

Azure said, "It was lucky you hadn't told him who you really were. I'm sorry you had to get involved. I know you hated the idea."

Maybe, Amber thought, she should have stood firm in her initial shocked refusal, but Azure's denials had been very convincing, and since childhood Amber had taken seriously her role of elder sister, warning her younger sibling to look both ways when crossing the road, defending her in schoolyard scraps, and forever getting her out of trouble. A hard-to-break habit.

Benny pushed away the sippy cup, tipping it over. Righting it, Azure continued, "I'm really, really grateful you made him go away, Ammie."

From what Amber had seen of the man, it would take a team of wild horses to *make* Marco Salzano do anything. Whereas she herself had allowed her sister's reasoning to override her aghast objections, her deeply held principles and her better judgement.

The baby, who had been playing with his mother's hair, turned to Amber with a heart-melting dimpled grin.

A clutch of fear for him gave her a taste of Azure's terror when she'd learned of Marco Salzano's visit. "You could get a DNA test," she suggested.

Azure flatly vetoed that. "Rickie and I have only just got back together again. I daren't rock the boat. He'd go ballistic if he knew Marco was *here*. I *can't* ask him to take a test now!"

Amber had to concede the potential complications were horrendous. Surely Benny's welfare was the most important thing. "You didn't miss any of your pills before…?"

Azure didn't answer, apparently absorbed in adoring her son, making kissing noises that he tried to copy.

Amber's voice sharpened. "Azzie?"

Azure looked up impatiently. "Not really. Only it's difficult to keep track when you're travelling, changing time zones and everything. Do leave it alone, Amber!"

Amber bit her tongue. Too late now to berate her sister. It would only end in tears. Refusing another glass of wine, she was about to leave when Azure's husband came in, his good-looking face lighting up as Benny broke into a delighted chuckle, wriggled down to the floor and took a couple of shaky steps, then held up his arms to be lifted, and planted a sloppy kiss on Rickie's cheek.

They *were* so alike, surely Azure's certainty was justified. And with any luck Marco Salzano was already on his way back to Venezuela.

In fact Marco was in the bar of his hotel, having a couple of measured drinks and tantalised by the memory of the previous night.

After leaving the cramped flat with its cheap but rather charming décor and its infuriatingly inconsistent occupant, he'd almost booked a flight home. Something held him back, a niggling doubt that he couldn't quite pin down.

He'd tried to dismiss the persistent image of wide, startled eyes closing as his mouth found sweet feminine lips, and the memory of how surprisingly soft they'd been beneath his—an image not conducive to clear thinking.

The woman had lied the first night and been evasive on the second. She was a good actress—her bewilderment and fear when he'd brushed aside her futile pretence of not knowing him had seemed almost convincing, now that he thought about it. At the time he'd been preoccupied with finding his son.

He was inclined to believe the baby was fictitious—ridiculous to feel a pang of grief. Unless she'd had it adopted. Or worse, ended the pregnancy before the child was even born. Her figure was perfect, the skin between the skimpy top and shorts taut and unmarred by stretch marks. Anger heated his blood, along with another emotion aroused by the memory of her body, half-naked as it was, briefly coming in contact with his.

Deliberately he quelled both reactions. Emotion interfered with logical thought.

Why, after that begging letter, had she refused his money with something like horror? Nothing added up. In his experience two and two always made four. If not, he wanted to know why, and invariably something in the equation was wrong—a mistake or a deliberate obfuscation.

He had told the desk clerk he was extending his stay—a decision readily accepted. Marco Salzano didn't flaunt his wealth but he had never been ungenerous with it.

After spending the morning making expensive telephone calls and checking his e-mail, he had studied the phone book in his room and later interviewed a private investigator.

Marco had given him as much information as would be needed to do a background check on Azure Odell, vaguely suggesting she was suspected of fraud.

"Can't do much today, but I'll get onto it tomorrow," the detective promised, "since you say it's urgent."

And since Marco had laid down a handsome initial fee. Now all he could do was wait.

Moodily he swilled the wine in his glass, ignoring the chatter in the crowded hotel bar and avoiding the eyes of two women perched on high stools that showed off their legs, who had been covertly inspecting him for some time.

For almost two years he'd put out of his mind the memory of that single night shared with a stranger, scarcely remembering the details. Yet now, after meeting her again, his body seemed to have a memory of its own—and an inconvenient desire to repeat the experience.

She was an attractive woman, even beautiful. But the women of his own country were renowned for their beauty. There was something else about her, some indefinable quality that eluded his mind yet appealed to his senses. Something he'd missed during that first casual encounter. Because now he couldn't seem to get her out of his mind, couldn't stop his body growing hot and restless.

He scowled at an open portfolio of papers lying on the table in front of him, a clear sign that he was working and didn't want company, but for fifteen minutes he'd stared at the printed sheets without comprehension. Idly scanning the room again, his gaze chanced upon the two women at the counter. Neither evoked a flicker of interest.

Next morning he breakfasted early before returning to his room. It was too soon to expect a call from the investigator, but that didn't stop him staring balefully at the light on the phone that refused to obligingly blink.

He killed time checking e-mail and researching the New Zealand beef industry on his computer, noting possible contacts if he should be here for a few more days. It was afternoon when the man contacted him. "The lessee of the address you gave me is an *Amber* Odell," he said. "Single, twenty-seven, works for a film and TV company in the city. She does apparently have a sister named Azure, but—"

"A sister?" Marco queried sharply.

"Yeah. She—the sister—doesn't live at that address."

"A twin?"

"Uh, don't think so. I could find out, get her address. It might take a bit longer if she's married and changed her name, but which woman are you interested in? Or is it both?"

"Yes—no." There was a faster way. "You have the address of this…Amber's…workplace?"

After putting down the phone Marco swore in his mother tongue, left his chair to pace the floor and swear some more, opened the bar fridge, then slammed it shut. This whole thing had started because for once he'd gone over his usual strict limit. He had to think. To control his first instinct, which was to find the woman, whatever her real name was, and wring her smooth, graceful, deceitful neck!

He wouldn't, of course, do that. But, he vowed, disciplining his hot, out-of-control rage to a contained, ruthless anger, he would see that she paid in full.

No one played Marco Salzano for a fool and got away with it. Not even a beautiful woman who set his blood on fire.

He consulted a map and found the street address the investigator had given him for the film studio. Marco's lip curled. Wasn't the film industry notorious for its casual attitude to sex? Like sister, like sister. *Amber* Odell had probably had dozens of lovers.

His gut tightened. Why should it matter how many men she had slept with? Especially if he wasn't, after all, one of them? The only reason for his driving need to see her was to find his son. Who surely did exist. Obviously the two sisters had cooked up that charade he'd been subjected to.

* * *

Leaving the Filmografia building in central Auckland, Amber stopped dead when Marco Salzano loomed in front of her, his face looking as if some sculptor had chiselled it out of unyielding rock. In his eyes was the banked fire of the anger he'd displayed at their first encounter.

"Hello, *Amber,*" he said, with dark, steely mockery in his tone.

"What are you doing here?" she gasped, her heart contracting into a shrivelled ball. "How did you find me?" She looked about her, but most of her colleagues had either already left or were still working. Filming wasn't the kind of business where working hours were cast in stone.

His expression changed slightly, as if she'd just satisfied him in some way. "We must talk."

He took her arm but she shook off his hand. "I don't need to talk to you," she said, trying to sidestep him, but this time he caught her arm in an unshakeable grip, trying to walk her along with him.

"Come, we cannot discuss anything here."

"I'm not going anywhere with you. Let go of me or I'll scream. Someone will call the police and I'll tell them you're stalking me." She opened her mouth and he dropped his hand from her arm, looking grimly amused.

"And I will tell them you are attempting to deprive me of my legal rights by fraud and deception. I'm not stalking you. I merely wish to talk about your sister."

Her *sister?* Of course, he'd called her by her own name, which she'd automatically reacted to. Not Azure's. How much did he know? "How did you find out where I work?"

"I hired an investigator," he said calmly.

"You…?" For a second she was stunned as well as angry. The idea of a stranger prying into her life gave her the creeps. "How dare you!"

"How else could I discover the truth? You lied to me."

"I didn't," she protested unconvincingly, her conscience stabbing. "I told you over and over you had the wrong person."

"*Sí.* The first time I came to your apartment. But the next evening you did not deny you had slept with me, written to me."

"What would be the point?" she said, pushing away a wildly inappropriate mental picture of herself and Marco in the same bed. "You'd jumped to a conclusion, and trying to set you straight hadn't worked before. I figured nothing I said was going to convince you."

"You did not say, *My sister* slept with you in Caracas and had your baby."

"How do you know there's a baby?" Her stomach went hollow.

Marco said, "Why else would you have played out that absurd pretence?"

Oh, hell! "Azure's *married*." Surely he could understand that no married woman wanted a previous lover turning up on her doorstep?

He said, "To the boyfriend who abandoned her in a foreign city full of men who had been drinking heavily?"

"It was a misunderstanding." She was tempted to remind him that by his own admission he'd been one of those men.

Carnaval in Caracas is just so wild! Azure had said. *People dancing on the streets wearing fantastic costumes, and drinking like there's no tomorrow. We were in an outdoor bar, and this skank in nothing but make-up and a few feathers dragged Rickie up to dance. He didn't even resist. And enjoyed it far too much. We had a fight and he went off in a huff, but I was sure he'd be back as soon as he calmed down. I was sitting there all alone with a bottle of wine, and a guy in a devil costume came on to me, wouldn't take no for an answer. I was getting scared when Marco came along and got rid of him. I knew Marco was someone important because the staff treated him like he was a lord or something. And we...started talking.*

And more. Amber shut that part off.

"Her fiancé walked off to calm himself down," she relayed to Marco, "but then he got lost in the crowd and couldn't find his way back." Or even remember the name of the bar, and had been both contrite and frantic when in the early hours he and Azure were finally reunited at their hotel. "They shared their cell phone, so he couldn't call her."

Two hours after Rickie went off, Azure had told her, I was still waiting and I was so mad at him! Marco's a very sexy man. We'd polished off another couple of bottles of wine and, well, one thing led to another.

"She made a mistake," Amber told him now.

"You too made a mistake," he accused her. "Don't imagine I will be so easily deceived again."

"Please—she's happy now and the baby's happy."

"I will be happy also, if she proves it is not mine."

"She said she's certain he isn't!"

"And you believe her?"

Amber hesitated for a fatal second and saw his eyes narrow, his jaw tighten. She said, "Surely she should know?"

Two young women came out of the building. "Hi, Amber," one said, and they paused, obviously angling for an introduction. "We're going to Cringles for a drink with the usual crowd. Want to come along and bring your friend?"

Amber was unwillingly fascinated by the way Marco Salzano's demeanour instantly changed. He gave the other women a dazzling smile and a slight inclination of his head. "You are kind, but please excuse us," he said. "Amber is about to join me for a drink and a private discussion."

They looked both smitten and disappointed, and one mouthed *Lucky you!* at Amber as they turned away.

Marco had taken her arm again and he said rapidly under his breath, "Your sister cannot avoid me forever. This time you will tell me the truth."

Amber stiffened but remained mute. He loosened his hold. "If you prefer we will talk in a public place. My hotel is within walking distance. There is a small bar there that I have noticed is not crowded at this time."

Amber allowed him to steer her to the street. Somehow she had to persuade him to leave Azure alone. Her brain was telling her this was Azure's problem. She should just say so and tell her sister to sort it out. But it wasn't only Azure who would pay for her brief folly. "All right," she said at last.

At the hotel Marco headed for a bar tucked discreetly into a corner on the ground floor. Only a few people were sitting in tub chairs at the round tables.

Amber asked for a glass of white wine and sipped it cautiously as Marco picked up his red. He'd also ordered a plate of taco chips with sour cream and sweet chilli sauce and gestured for her to help herself before he took one.

Amber's taste buds awoke at the sight of the platter, and as Marco washed his mouthful down with a sip of wine she thought how oddly intimate it was to share food with a man she couldn't help thinking of as the enemy.

He put down his glass and regarded her with his head tipped slightly back, his eyes hooded. She recalled the smile he'd directed at her friends, not at all the way he looked at her, glaring with anger and suspicion.

She said, "My sister didn't say her baby was yours." Surely Azure hadn't lied to her about that.

His lip curled. "If she did not intend me to think so, why did she suggest I would be willing to give her thousands of dollars for the sake of the child?"

Amber inwardly winced. Azure did tend to rush into things without thinking. Her family had hoped that marriage and motherhood might temper that trait. "Desperation," she suggested.

"So?" he said scornfully.

"She…she'd told her husband about what happened in Caracas, and he was upset…angry." Sometimes Amber thought Azure and her husband were too alike. It hadn't been the first time in their long relationship that they'd temporarily split after a quarrel. But she supposed no other had been caused by such a devastating revelation. Certainly none had lasted so long.

Marco frowned. "Is he violent?"

"Oh no! No. But he left her and she panicked."

He said Benny might be anybody's, Azure had sobbed, finally confessing to her sister why Rickie hadn't been around for a while. Previously she'd told her family he was working out of town. The big industrial electrical firm that had employed him covered a wide area, and it wasn't unusual for him to be away for a few days. *He said he wasn't coming back. His family say they don't know where he is. He even left his job.*

"Then her marriage is no more?" Marco asked sharply. "The child is without a father?"

"No. He missed her, and the baby. He loves them both so much. After almost two months he came back. Azure asked if he wanted a DNA test and he said no."

Thinking she saw a flicker of disbelief in Marco's expression, she said passionately, "He's the only father the baby's ever known, and they're good parents. It would be cruel to take Benny from them. Cruel to him. And it would break my sister's heart." She couldn't keep the tremor from her voice, her eyes from stinging.

Azure's greatest fear was not losing her husband again, although Amber knew she'd be devastated, but that Marco Salzano would want to take Benny from her. *People with that much money can do anything!* she'd cried. *Pay top lawyers. Even kidnap him! Kidnapping's a business in South America.*

It was true other children had been spirited off illegally to a different country, some never returned.

Amber too loved Benny, and the thought of him being snatched away made her own heart ache unbearably. How much worse would it be for her sister?

Marco said, "The boy is very young. I have a right—" apparently confirming her worst fear.

"He has rights too! Who knows how a tiny baby feels about being torn from its mother's arms, taken from everything he's used to—what long-term effects it has?"

"You are being melodramatic. I don't mean to—"

Amber ignored that. "You can't possibly feel the same way they do. You've never even seen him." Repeating all the arguments Azure had used to persuade her to go along with Marco's mistaken identification of her sister.

"That is why I'm here," he said. "To see him. And should he be mine—"

"He *isn't* yours! If Azure hadn't written that stupid letter you'd never have known he existed."

"If she didn't want me to know, why did she write it?"

Momentarily Amber closed her eyes. If only... But it was spilt milk now. "Her husband had gone, she thought forever, maybe to Australia or further, and he hadn't paid the mortgage installment due on their house. Every cent they had—" Amber knew that hadn't been much "—went into buying it. My parents helped, and they guaranteed the loan. If the bank foreclosed, they would have lost their home too."

His frown deepened. "It was foolish of them to do so."

Her voice sharpening at the criticism, she said, "Parents will do anything for their children. Or grandchildren. Even if they're not lucky enough to have a family fortune." Her father had retired and sold his country house and farm contracting business after a heart attack, moving into a small town house that ate up nearly all the proceeds. "You don't know what it's like not to have a lot of money. Or how it would feel to lose a child."

A spasm seemed to cross Marco's harsh features. He took a moment to compose himself, rearrange his face into a grim mask. "You are wrong," he said, his voice almost expressionless. "I have lost a child. My seven-year-old son died some years ago, along with his mother, my wife."

CHAPTER FOUR

AMBER'S breath stuck in her throat. She could feel her face going cold, then hot. Marco had been married? Had a child? Children, perhaps. "I'm so *sorry*," she said, stricken. "I had no idea."

He shrugged, apparently in total control of himself. "How should you? Your sister and I did not talk about such private things during our brief…liaison. But the day we met was the anniversary of their deaths." Only a slight thickening of his voice suggested emotion. "I had been persuaded by friends to join them for the festival. They meant well, but I was not in the mood, and when we became parted I had no desire to find them and continue celebrating. Instead I kept drinking on my own. A mistake. And continued to drink with your sister—more than I realised at the time. Another mistake."

"I'm sorry," Amber said again, "about your family. Do you—did you and your wife have other children?"

"No. She had a difficult pregnancy and the birth was also not easy. I was not willing to see her suffer like that again. But the boy…" His tone softened, and in his eyes Amber saw both pleasure and pain. "The boy was remarkably healthy, quick to learn, but also loving, affectionate, like his mother. And always laughing." He stopped, and his hand went to his heart for a moment before dropping to the table.

"No," he amended, shaking his head, "that is not true of any child. Sometimes he wept—even roared." Briefly amusement mingled with sorrow in the dark eyes. "He had a temper, like his father." The beautiful male mouth curved self-deprecatingly at the admission. "But that is how I remember him. Laughing."

Amber was unable to speak. This aspect of Marco Salzano she would never have expected. A loving, grieving father.

Marco picked up his glass and drained it, then turned to signal a waiter for more. "What about you?" he asked, nodding at her half-empty glass.

Amber shook her head, and took a couple of tacos to hide her reaction. They seemed to lodge in her throat so she drank some more wine. She didn't feel she could ask how Marco's son and his wife had died. An accident?

He had banished the sadness from his eyes. Now they were neutral, all emotion hidden. Obviously he wanted to dismiss the subject.

But didn't this change everything?

A man who had lost his only child and then thought he'd been presented with another wasn't simply selfish and possessive. His insistence on seeing the little boy was understandable.

Yet so was Azure's fear of losing her baby.

Amber's loyalty must be with her sister. Marco had uncovered their deception, but was he still hell-bent on seeing Benny? And if he did, would he even try to resist a natural urge to claim him and take him home?

The waiter brought more wine, but instead of drinking, Marco turned it with his fingers on the stem of the glass, his eyes lowered so Amber couldn't guess at his thoughts.

Again Azure's voice echoed in her head, high with panic, while tears ran down her cheeks. *Over there men are in charge of everything—the family, business, politics... Their laws might even favour the father. Especially if he's as rich and respected as Marco Salzano.*

Amber's own foray onto the Internet to look up international law had turned up nothing reassuring. Even though Venezuela was signatory to an international convention on child custody, it appeared to have had little effect.

To Marco, Amber said, "Even if he *were* yours, think about the baby."

"I could give him everything a child needs."

"Everything?" She let her scepticism show. "He has a loving mother and father now. Two parents. What would you do—hire a nanny? And when she left, another one? Set up a pattern for the poor kid of being loved and left...or taken away?"

He picked up a taco, but instead of eating it began stabbing it into the sour cream until it disintegrated. Scowling, he wiped his fingers on a red paper napkin.

Only then he looked at her and said, "I would love him. And ensure he is well and happy. If necessary I may marry again, if I find someone suitable."

"To give him a mother? He already has one. Pity the poor woman you marry for expediency."

"She would be very well cared for, have everything she wants."

"Except your love."

"Love has many faces."

"If you want to show love for this...this *barely possible* child of yours, the best thing to do is to go away and forget about him."

He searched her face. "You truly believe this?"

"His mother and father adore him. They are good people. Not rich, but he'll be well looked after."

"His 'father' left them apparently without a penny, about to be thrown out of their home. That is irresponsible."

"It was a mistake."

His mouth twisted again into a sneer. "Yet another mistake?"

"He'd changed his job, arranged for the mortgage money to be taken out of his wages when they were banked by his employer, but someone slipped up and the payment was delayed. He explained it all to Azure when he came home and told her he couldn't live without her...and their baby."

His eyes flashed at the last few words. "His mother is a liar and an extortionist, and she cheated on her husband. A court may not see them as fit parents for my child."

"You make her sound like a criminal! She's not. And she and Rickie weren't married when...when they were in Venezuela! And it was the only time she slept with anyone else."

"You cannot be sure of that."

"That's what she said, and I believe her. They've hardly been apart since they met in high school."

His expression showed scepticism again, cynicism. "They took a long time to marry."

"These days people are marrying later, sometimes after they've lived together for years. I don't know about your country, but it's common here." Her parents had opposed a teenage marriage, and later, Amber suspected, regretted it when the couple appeared to have shelved the idea in favour of travelling the world. "They were married seven months before the baby was born."

Marco was still twirling the glass, then he picked it up and drank, one gulp. "I insist on a DNA test," he said.

* * *

"No!" Azure clutched Benny to her breast as though Marco were there in person, about to snatch him away.

"Why not?" Again Amber was sitting in her sister's kitchen. She'd promised Marco that she would relay his demand in return for his assurance that he wouldn't approach Benny's mother. "If Rickie really is the biological father you have nothing to worry about."

"I can't." Azure's eyes were wide, afraid. "I won't."

"But you offered Rickie—"

"Dig it all up again? Risk our marriage a second time? Rickie was there when I had Benny, he was the first one to hold him, even before me. He's got up in the night to change him, feed him, walk him back to sleep when he's fussing. Benny adores him! It's Rickie's name on the birth certificate, and anyway, legally a woman's husband is the father of her baby. I checked."

"Really? Surely if another man can prove—"

"Prove *what?*" Azure cried. "That by some biological freak accident, a thousand-to-one chance, another man's sperm produced my child? Rickie's his *real* father."

Amber said, "Wouldn't it be better to know for sure?"

Vehemently Azure shook her head. "Rickie said Benny is his son and nothing can change that, and it's true. *It's true.*" Sobbing, she buried her lips in Benny's fragile neck, while tears dampened his tiny blue shirt. "This is all my fault and it isn't *fair* to make them suffer for it."

Amber rose from her chair and swiftly enclosed both mother and baby in her arms. "Maybe the test could be done without Rickie knowing. If you're right, there's nothing to worry about, Marco will leave." Inside her something trembled. "You said it's a thousand-to-one chance."

"*No*. I won't do that behind Rickie's back. *I* would know. And if…if it did turn out wrongly…" Her anguished eyes teared up again. "I couldn't bear it! Please, Amber, make him go *away!*"

The final wail sounded exactly like six-year-old Azure begging her nine-year-old sister to chase away the monsters under the bed. Amber had invented an invincible magic spell to banish them and persuaded the smaller girl to see for herself that the monsters had disappeared.

She didn't think there was any magic that would force Marco Salzano to disappear.

"I will come now," Marco said when she phoned his hotel and asked to see him, hoping a face-to-face meeting would be more persuasive than a telephone conversation. "Unless you prefer to meet me here?"

"I'll meet you at the hotel," she said. Neutral ground. And last time they had talked there, they'd managed to come to some sort of agreement.

He met her in the lobby, which was milling with people. "We'll have to talk in my suite," he said. "There's some kind of convention going on."

People wearing name tags occupied every sofa and chair in sight, and both bars buzzed, standing room only.

"I'm sorry," Marco said. "I did not realise earlier. They must have been in meetings, but now…" As Amber hesitated he added, "You will be quite safe."

"I know," she said quickly. Although she'd never felt really safe with Marco Salzano, she was certain he wouldn't normally offer deliberate violence to a woman. Still, something deep inside her whispered as they ascended in the lift to his floor that if he offered her another kiss like the one he'd pressed on her before…

The doors swept apart and she stepped out, burying the wayward thought. Tonight he hadn't touched her, except for a light hand at her waist as they crossed to the elevator—a natural courtesy, she supposed, for a man like him. Even that had sent tiny shivers of awareness along her spine. She wondered if all his compatriots shared that potent aura of rampant masculinity.

The suite was predictably luxurious, a king-size bed visible through an open door from the main room. On a polished desk a laptop computer had its screen open, printed papers beside it. A mobile phone seemed to be connected to the computer.

"You've been working?" Amber couldn't hide her surprise.

"The Internet is a wonderful invention." Marco motioned her to a chair before seating himself at the other side of a low round table that held two wine bottles and glasses, and a plate of savoury nibbles. "It is possible to conduct some of my business while I am away from home."

"I thought…" She stopped there.

"You thought?" he queried, lifting one of the bottles.

"That you'd no need to work," she said, a little embarrassed.

"You imagine, perhaps, that I spend my time playing polo and partying?"

"I hadn't really thought about it. I have no idea how you spend your time."

He held up the bottle. "You asked for white last time. I ordered a white and a red, both New Zealand wines that the hotel sommelier assures me are excellent. But if you prefer something else I can have room service bring it."

"I'm sure that will be fine." She nodded at the bottle.

He poured and sat back, picking up the conversation. "I run a large *hato* belonging to my family. We run a tourist business and raise beef for export. You would call it a ranch."

Amber shook her head. "That's North American. Here we'd probably call it a cattle station."

"Station? Ah." He smiled, nodded as though absorbing the information. "We have other business and community responsibilities also. Since my father died I have been in charge."

"We?"

"I have two sisters, one with children, and my mother. Also uncles and cousins who have a financial interest in the family holdings."

"It sounds like an empire."

He laughed, and it transformed his face, making him look younger, happy. Something tugged at her heart, and she remembered the grief she'd seen when he talked about his dead son. Was this how he had been before that tragedy?

He said, "I am no emperor. Merely a hardworking *llanero*. A cowboy," he translated, and then smiled as at a small joke. He certainly didn't look like any cowboy she'd ever imagined. "Also," he added, "of necessity, we have various irons in the fire. It is unwise in these times to put all your eggs in one basket."

"Your English is very good." He had even mastered the clichés.

"I spent some time in the United States as a teenager, learning how they run their cattle industry and picking up a few other things."

He looked at her over his glass, the light falling through the big windows catching on the rich red of the wine, making golden shimmers. "Your sister—" he said "—has she agreed to have the baby tested?"

Amber tensed, looking down into her glass, then took a quick swallow for Dutch courage. "She…she said no."

Rushing on, she reiterated Azure's objections, making them as persuasive as she could. "Try to see it her way," she begged, seeing Marco's face set into austere lines. "A few hours with you compared with a lifetime—she hopes—with her husband. It's too late for you to claim the baby now, even if he does share your DNA. He belongs to Azzie."

Marco's expression didn't change, and she couldn't read what he was thinking. She went on, praying to get through to him. "Azure nurtured him in her own body for nine months, brought him into the world, and she'll do *anything* to keep him safe and happy. She was wrong to sleep with you, wrong not to be more careful. But she isn't the only one to blame, and removing him now from his parents, his home, his country, won't make it right."

Marco got up, taking his wine with him to stand at the window, looking out to where the lights of the city reflected into the dark harbour.

Amber realised her hands were clenched hard in her lap.

Marco made a small movement and she held her breath, but he didn't turn. "I believe I could get a court order," he said, still without looking at her, "to enforce a test."

So he'd been doing some research too. She got up and walked over to him. Only then did he swing round to face her. She said, "You loved your son who died, must have wanted what was best for him. But you can't replace a person with another one. I know you still grieve for your little boy. Can you inflict that grief on a mother—and a father—who feel the same about their…about this child?"

His mouth finally softened slightly from its fiercely held line. "You are a passionate advocate," he said. "Your sister is fortunate you are so eager to plead for her."

"You don't know how terrified she is," Amber said. "If you could see how much she loves Ben—"

He lifted his free hand and put his fingers over her mouth, silencing her. "Enough."

She didn't understand the way he was looking at her, even after he dropped his hand to his side. "Wha-what are you going to do?" she asked, dreading to hear the answer.

His voice sounded odd, very deep and a little blurred. He was staring at her face as though memorising it. "I cannot give you an answer now," he said. "It is not a matter to be decided on a whim."

Amber swallowed any protest she might have made. He was right; it was asking a lot of a man. Especially this man, who had suffered the loss of his family and then discovered he might have an unknown child. She nodded. "I understand."

"I doubt it." A dry note that had become familiar reappeared in his tone.

"I suppose that was a stupid thing to say." How could she possibly know, who had never had a child herself?

"I don't think you are stupid," Marco said. "Loyal, perhaps to the point of folly. Compassionate…loving. You and your sister are close? And also, you are beautiful."

Amber brushed off the last bit as Latin hyperbole. "Azure and I are very close. There's only the two of us."

"You are very alike."

She nodded. "But if you'd known my baby sister better, you wouldn't have mistaken me for her."

"Baby?" His brows rose.

In his eyes of course Azure was very much a woman. She'd even given birth, a rite of passage to womanhood that was more than Amber could claim.

Perhaps it was time to let her sister fight her own battles.

But despite her initial reluctance she didn't regret taking part in this one. "I should go," she said. "You will think about…all this?"

"I have thought about little else since I arrived in this country."

"And please," she added, "don't do anything before telling me what you've decided?"

"In return for a promise from you," he said.

"Oh?" Cautiously she asked, "What?"

"Two promises. One, that you will not spirit the child away, nor help your sister do so. And two…have dinner with me one night. Tomorrow, perhaps?"

"I'm busy tomorrow night." She'd been invited to a hen party for an old school friend.

"When?" he asked, leaving it to her.

"Well, Monday night is free." Was this a date, or did he have some kind of negotiations in mind? He'd called her beautiful. Again that kiss came to the front of her consciousness, in all its mind-blowing delight. If he planned to follow up on it…

A stirring of anticipation made her step back. That wouldn't do! The sooner this disturbing, far-too-attractive man went back to Venezuela the better.

"Don't look so worried." He smiled, and she felt her response like a ray of sunshine entering her body. She'd seen the effect of that smile on other women, but now he'd turned it on her she thought Azure would have had to be superhuman to resist it. "Finish your wine," he said, "before you leave me to my thoughts."

"I've had enough." She was relieved that her voice didn't sound breathless. "Thank you, it was very good."

He followed her to the door and leaned forward to open it for her, giving her a whiff of his subtle masculine scent.

"I will phone," he promised, and brushed his lips across her cheek before stepping back.

A current of electricity of some kind seemed to shoot through her, not painful but wickedly pleasurable. She stood looking at him, her lips parted in astonishment.

A glow in his dark eyes held her for a moment.

"Good night," she said in a muffled voice.

As the elevator carried her to the ground floor she tried to analyse what had happened then. She'd never experienced anything like it before. Did the man carry some sort of secret high-tech gadget that he used to extraordinary effect on women? Highly unlikely.

A man like that, who emanated sex appeal from metres away without even looking at a woman, hardly needed any help, electronic or otherwise. But he threatened to ruin her sister's life. She'd be mad to let him into hers.

All weekend, with a mixture of dread and something like the feeling she'd had as a kid on Christmas Eve, Amber kept thinking of the coming Monday. On Sunday she visited Azure and watched Rickie playing with Benny. When Rickie picked him up and held him high the baby was totally unafraid, giggling back at his grinning father until Rickie hugged him close and planted a smacking kiss on his rounded cheek.

Amber's throat ached. Glancing at her sister, she saw the haunted look in Azure's eyes behind her smile.

When she got home the phone was ringing and she caught it in her bedroom before the answer machine kicked in.

"Are you all right?" a deep masculine voice asked when she'd breathlessly answered.

"Yes, I just got in." Her heart quickened its pace.

"Ah," Marco said. "I tried several times to reach you."

"You could have left a message on the answer machine."

"I didn't want to talk with a machine. I wished to hear your voice."

A strange sensation travelled from her throat to her diaphragm, and her hand tightened on the receiver.

"Are you there?" Marco demanded.

"Yes."

"Tomorrow night," he said. "I will come to fetch you—"

"No!" It was instinctive. Already her home was haunted by the memory of his forceful presence. Each time she entered her sitting room she recalled his formidable expression when he accused her of lying, the leaping flame in his eyes before he kissed her. And when she glanced at Azure and Benny's photograph on her dressing table she remembered shielding it with her body from Marco's probing gaze while she prayed he wouldn't see it.

When he spoke again his voice had regained the harsh, implacable note it had carried that night. "We had a bargain," he said. "An agreement."

"I meant, don't pick me up. I'll meet you."

In the pause that followed she somehow knew he was scowling. "Very well," he said at last, the clipped tone conveying his displeasure. "Does seven-thirty suit you? I will meet you in the lobby of my hotel and we will get a cab. I have been told of a very good restaurant in Parnell."

The restaurant was fabulous. Amber was glad she had dressed up a little, in a peacock-blue silk dress with a swathed bodice and wide, low neckline that showed off a paua-shell pendant, carved into one of the intricate spirals favoured by Maori artists. The swirling blues and greens of the polished shell perfectly complemented the dress.

They were led to a table across thick carpet that sank

under her high heels. The waiter seated her in a velvet-up-holstered chair, presented a large leather-backed menu, shook out the intricate folds of the white napkin standing upright in front of her and laid it on her lap, then did the same for Marco.

Occasionally with friends she'd splurged for a special treat on something more expensive than pizza or cheap ethnic cafés. She had dated actors trying to impress her after snagging a highly paid advertisement or feature film role.

This was way out of her experience. She had heard of the restaurant and the eccentric genius of the chef who owned it. But she'd never entered its august portals within one of the refurbished heritage buildings that made Parnell a haunt of tourists and wealthy locals.

If Marco had hoped to impress her, she reluctantly conceded that he had. But this was probably everyday for him. She supposed he was used to expecting and getting the best and was prepared to pay for it.

She looked across the damask-covered table and asked, "Are you going to tell me what you've decided?"

"Later," he said. "Let us enjoy our meal first."

Amber wasn't sure she could enjoy anything with that vital decision still hanging fire, but he smiled at her and said, "Please relax, Amber. Worrying will spoil your appetite, and there is no need."

Did that mean he'd given up his quest? Strangely the idea brought with it a hollow feeling mingled with the leap of hope. Contradictory and confusing.

He was perusing the menu and she turned her attention to hers. Already she knew he wasn't to be cajoled into changing his mind. If he didn't want to talk now she would have to wait.

They had drinks while waiting for their order, and

Marco kept the conversation light, asking questions about New Zealand life and people, querying her about her job. She told him anecdotes about her research work and the world of film and TV, and once or twice he laughed, giving her a frisson of half-guilty pleasure. It didn't seem right to be enjoying Marco Salzano's company.

The food when it came was perfectly presented, perfectly cooked, and the wines Marco chose in consultation with the wine waiter complemented each dish, also to perfection.

Amber didn't finish all her wines, served in huge glasses. She was wary of the effect alcohol might have on her. Marco ate and drank with relish and appreciation, obviously savouring the various tastes, but had only one glass of each wine.

Over a light dessert she asked him about Venezuela and watched a new expression come into his eyes as he described growing up on the vast grasslands of the Los Llanos district—riding horses and helping to muster cattle, and from the age of twelve helping conduct tours of his ancestral land. It was—without exaggeration, she gathered—the size of a small country. Pumas, jaguars, monkeys, ocelots and some animal called capybara still roamed its plains and jungles.

"Many of our wild animals are endangered species," he said. "Eco-tourism is big business for Venezuela. Our *hato* has been a wildlife reserve for the past thirty-four years, and we don't allow hunting."

"What about your cattle? How do they co-exist?"

"We lose a few to the big cats. But cattle make little impact on the land. In some places we have made canals to trap water for them, and the wild animals share in that."

After they'd finished eating he pushed away his plate, laid his forearms on the table and fixed his gaze on her. "I have, as you suggested, given this matter much thought. But—" he looked around at the other diners, mostly businessmen entertaining one another, or parties of the young and rich who were becoming rather raucous "—perhaps this is not the right place. We can have coffee at my hotel. And afterwards I will send you home."

She thought about it, then nodded. "All right."

The hotel was quieter now, and they sat in a dimly lit corner of the small bar, away from the few other patrons. Tense again, Amber picked up a white marshmallow from her cappuccino's saucer and let it melt in her mouth.

Marco seemed in no hurry, stirring sugar into his coffee. Then he put down the spoon and drummed long, lean fingers on the table for a couple of seconds before looking up. "You may be right," he said, "that the boy is best left with your sister and her husband."

Relief washed over her, and impulsively she stretched out her own hand and laid it on his. "Oh, thank you! It *is* the right thing, though I know it's hard for you."

Suddenly conscious of the warm, tensile strength of his hand, she made to withdraw hers, but with a lightning-fast movement he caught her fingers, almost crushing them before his hold eased a little.

"Wait," he said. "There are conditions."

Caution took the place of relief. "What conditions?"

For a moment he didn't speak. His thumb was, apparently absently, caressing her skin, which reacted to the slight roughness of his, giving off tiny, invisible sparks. He looked down and said, "I wish to make you a proposition." Then he raised his eyes to hers, darkly probing as if trying to enter her mind.

Amber stiffened. His English, although formal, was fluent—he must know the word had more than one meaning.

She tugged at her hand, and this time he released it. Her heart hammered unevenly. Emotions and thoughts tumbled over each other—anger, dread, a piercing and puzzling disappointment, hope that she was mistaken, and a shameful stirring of something too much like excitement.

His expression turned to amusement. "Not that," he said. "You think I would insult you so?"

Mortified, and annoyed that he could read her so easily, she said more sharply than she'd intended, "What, then?"

"Your sister's letter," he told her, "said nothing about a husband. I understood she was a single mother."

"At the time—"

"I know." He held up a hand, then went on. "I hoped that if she was not willing to give up her child I might persuade her to marry me and return with me to my home."

Amber's mouth opened and closed again.

He said, "It seemed the most practical solution. For the child's sake. Then you told me her husband had returned. And you begged me to leave them alone."

He paused again, and she said, "What do you want?" What conditions did he have in mind that would persuade him to do that? Foreboding filled her.

"I want *you*," he said with quiet implacability. As she recoiled, he captured her hand again, saying rapidly, "Not as my mistress, Amber. I want you to marry me. And give me a child."

CHAPTER FIVE

AMBER sat stunned. Marry Marco Salzano? After several seconds she managed to croak out, "You can't be serious!"

The room—the whole world—seemed to recede into some distant sphere, leaving them isolated in a dizzying vacuum. The only reality was herself and Marco, his eyes intense and without a hint of irony or teasing.

"I do not offer women marriage for a joke," he said. "I am very serious."

Shock beginning to recede, her brain returned to something resembling working order, and a creeping cold assailed her body.

Of course he hadn't fallen madly in love with her in the course of a week or so. He was suggesting a solution to an insoluble problem—a monstrous solution. With herself as some kind of female sacrifice. "That's…it's blackmail," she said.

He frowned. "It is negotiation. You are at liberty to refuse, but that is my offer."

From icy cold she'd gone to raging mad. "A convenient marriage and a substitute child?"

"You are angry." Stating the obvious. "Why?"

"Why?" Angry didn't begin to describe what she felt. "What did you expect? That I'd be flattered?"

His back straightened and his head lifted, his proud *hidalgo* ancestry coming to the fore. "It is not an insult to be asked to marry a Salzano."

"You didn't ask! You *demanded.* As the price of…of…"

"Of my giving up my son." He looked immovable. "I do not think it is too high a price."

"He's not your son!" She leaned forward to emphasise the words.

"I do not know that. However, if you accept my proposal I swear I will relinquish any claim to him except that of a fond uncle. Has he been baptised?"

"What?" The change of subject threw her.

"Does he have godparents? I would like to—"

"Yes!" she answered. "I'm one. And Rickie's brother."

"Then I will be an honorary godfather as your husband."

"You are *not* going to be my husband! You're out of your mind! Find yourself another brood mare."

She pushed back her chair, swept up her wallet and keys, and stalked towards the lobby, then outside where several taxis waited for custom. Sliding into one, she discovered that Marco had been right behind her and was in beside her before she'd even closed her door.

Instinctively she moved away from him, saying between her teeth, "Get out!" But her voice was drowned by his deep one giving the driver her address.

"He's not with me!" she told the driver.

The man turned. "Sir? If the lady—"

Marco said to him in a man-to-man, indulgent tone, "We had a quarrel, but she will get over it."

"Ma'am?" the driver queried. "That's your address?"

"Yes, but—"

"Give us a minute," Marco said. He turned to Amber. "I would prefer to continue our argument in private. When you calm down you will be able to see this more rationally. Is there not a saying, Never let the sun go down on anger?"

"The sun *is* down," she retorted. Childishly.

He gave a low laugh that inflamed her further. Wasn't that advice usually given to couples? *Married* couples.

His voice low, he said, "We agreed I would not contact your sister until I made a decision. I have decided. If you turn this down…" He shrugged.

Amber was silent. It seemed he really was serious.

The driver asked impatiently, "Are we moving or not? Do I turn on the meter?"

"All right," Amber said, defeated. "Yes."

She fastened her seat belt and tried to think rationally. Could she secretly take a sample of Benny's saliva, get it tested? Behind Azure's back and against her wishes?

What if he was Marco's child? All the reasons Azure gave for refusing the DNA test were valid, but if she were really certain he was Rickie's, surely she'd have agreed?

Stealing a peek at Marco's profile, she saw he looked grimly determined. This wasn't some spur-of-the-moment whim. He'd looked at the angles, weighed up the options and found a bargaining chip he could use, like the businessman he surely was. So much for hot-blooded Latin passion.

Suddenly she wanted to cry. For her nephew, her sister. Herself. Even for Marco. Her chest was tight, and something inside hurt in a way she could neither describe nor understand. She gazed blindly out of the window at the streetlights, the passing cars. She was still angry—furious. And wouldn't admit even to herself that the anger was largely fuelled by that hidden, aching hurt.

When they arrived at her apartment, Amber didn't even try to stop him coming inside. She switched on the sitting room light, dropped her wallet on a red-box side table and faced him. She didn't sit down and didn't invite him to, either. This was no cosy conversation.

She said, "You can't really expect me to give up my home, my family, my job. Even my country!"

"You will not need a job. Your family may visit as much as they wish. I will pay their fares if necessary. You may go home at any time—after you have my child."

"And leave him—her, whatever—with you?" There was no way she'd ever be able to do that. She even missed Benny if she'd been away from him for more than a week or two.

Marco shrugged, but she saw his jaw clamp tightly for a second. "It will be your choice. In my faith, marriage is for life, but I will not coerce you to stay. Nor forbid you to see the child whenever you wish."

"Oh, that's generous!"

"Perhaps," he said softly, "more than you know."

"Supposing I can't have children?" she demanded.

His brows drew together. "Do you have reason to believe you cannot?"

"No," she admitted. "But it happens."

"Then we will see what can be done. I should warn you, if I find you are deliberately cheating me, I will not be held by promises."

Amber couldn't believe they were actually discussing this. Of course she couldn't do it. This dilemma wasn't even her problem.

Then she remembered Benny's bright little face beaming at Azure and Rickie, thought of how her parents doted on their only grandchild, and felt a tug of pain at the idea of not having him in her own life. Her entire family would be devastated if Marco took him to South America. Rickie's, too; he had a large and loving whanau—his extended family.

"There must be another way," she muttered.

"You know the only way." As she stood there chewing on her lip, he crossed the carpet and said softly, "Don't torture your lovely mouth so."

She stopped the unconscious action.

His thumb soothed her stinging lip with a featherlike touch. He lifted her chin and equally gently kissed her mouth. It was so comforting, so tender that she didn't pull away instantly, liking it far too much before coming to her senses and stepping back, her whole body tingling.

"It will not be too difficult," he said, his voice a seduction in itself. "I promise I will be a considerate lover. My home is comfortable and well staffed, and my country has its own beauty. You will want for nothing."

The mention of a well-staffed home, so casually dropped, made her conscious of the enormous gap between their lifestyles. She wouldn't have any idea how to deal with servants. "I would never fit in," she blurted out.

"I assure you, my family will welcome my wife. My sisters have been urging me to marry again."

"Oh, stop!" she cried. Her hands going to her temples, she closed her eyes. Surely this was some idiotic dream. For one thing she was tempted to say yes, and in real life only insanity would have let her entertain for a millisecond the notion of marrying a stranger—a stranger who threatened her entire family.

But when she opened her eyes, Marco Salzano was still solidly real and present, reaching for her hands and pressing the right one to his chest so she could feel the beat of his heart, making her own increase its rhythm as he kissed her forehead, then quickly both cheeks.

"If you need time to consider," he said, his eyes like dark, liquid fire, mesmerising her, "I will wait." Then his mouth captured hers for a long moment, very lightly, as though he remembered her lower lip was still throbbing, and was being careful not to hurt her.

He stepped back and lifted her hands one by one, kissing each of them before releasing it. "But not too long," he said, before he turned and left her.

Standing like a living but scarcely breathing statue, Amber watched him go, heard the front door close behind him. Only then did she move, trying to shake off the alternately hot and then cold, shivery sensation that enveloped her.

"He's mad," she said aloud. And she'd be mad to even contemplate such a thing. Whatever they did in Venezuela, she reminded herself, heading for the bathroom as though walking underwater, a marriage of convenience—*his* convenience—was out of the question.

One of her friends had seriously considered marrying a gay friend so she could stay on in the United States after her visa ran out. Some people married for tax reasons.

That was different. She splashed her face several times with cold water, and was annoyed and dismayed at her reflection in the mirror. Her cheeks bore a faint flush, her lips were full and soft and red, and despite the harsh light the pupils of her eyes were huge.

She looked like a sleepwalker, but there was no doubt she was awake and aware.

She remained wakeful all night, alternately trying to find ways out of the impasse, and fantasising about being married to a man who with a mere look made her more conscious of her womanhood than she had ever been, and who could shatter her equilibrium with a brief touch of his lips on her cheek, her forehead, her hand, set her entire body on fire when he took her mouth under his with tenderness and consideration for a bruised lip.

Sex doesn't last, she told herself sternly, and for the nth time turned over in bed. Not at that level of intensity, anyway.

Then she remembered that his main interest in sex with her was to create a baby. A baby made to order.

She thumped a fist into her pillow, stared through the window at a sickle moon high in the sky. Marco found her sexually attractive, she knew. He had called her beautiful, and other things besides—loyal, compassionate and loving.

He too was surely capable of being all those things. He'd loved and grieved for his son and surely for his wife. Even after she died he'd apparently been in no hurry to remarry. He had shown concern when Amber felt sick that first night he'd come storming into her life like a dark avenging angel, and again tonight when he realised even before she did that in her agitation she was hurting herself.

Yet he was also capable of using her love for her family to force her into a loveless marriage. He was that ruthless in getting what he wanted.

But he'd promised to let her go once she had his baby.

Which left her without any romantic illusions. Once she'd fulfilled his need for an heir he wouldn't care if she left or stayed.

She closed her eyes, willing herself to sleep, but unable to banish from her mind Marco's intense, dark gaze, his gorgeous, sexy mouth and his deep, black-velvet voice with the hint of iron beneath its seductive cadence.

After work the next day she spent a couple of hours with colleagues in a nearby bar, celebrating the wrap of their current project. It didn't stop her thinking about Marco and his extraordinary offer, but it helped.

Having had a couple more glasses than usual she took

a bus, which dropped her a block from her home. When she opened the door her phone was ringing.

"Amber!" Azure's voice was hushed. "Did you talk to him again? What did he say?"

The extra alcohol made Amber reckless, and less tolerant of the sister who had got her into this. She said, "Marco? He asked me to marry him."

"What?" Azure squealed. Then in a hurried whisper, "That isn't funny."

"I'm not joking." Echoing his words. "He wants me to have his baby."

The silence at the other end was rather gratifying, although Amber knew it was unkind to feel that way. In the background she could hear baby squeals and splashing, and Rickie's laughter. He must be bathing Benny. It sounded as though they were both enjoying it.

Finally Azure said, "He can't mean it."

"Why not?" Amber asked airily, oddly annoyed. "He thinks I'm beautiful." Recklessly she added, "And actually I rather fancy him."

Azure gasped. "You *can't*, Amber. I won't *let* you! Don't you realise the only reason he's asked is to stay close to Benny? What do you mean, he wants you to have his baby?"

For some reason hearing Azure say what Amber already knew increased her irritation. She said, "He lives in Venezuela—that's hardly close. Do you want to change your mind about DNA testing?"

"What's that got to do with it? I told you, I'll never…" A pause, then, "Why are you asking?"

"Because he swears he'll never bother you and Benny if I give him a baby."

Azure was silent again for what seemed an age. Then

she said, seemingly shaken, "You can't marry a man like that. This is all my fault. I'll do whatever you want."

She sounded so defeated Amber's annoyance died.

"I'll have to tell Rickie first," Azure said unsteadily. "I don't know if our marriage will survive, but keeping this mess secret isn't worth ruining your life too. Thanks all the same, Amber, for trying. You're the best sister anyone could have."

"Wait!" Amber felt wretched now. "Azzie, I love you and I love Benny. Marco's not all that bad. You didn't know, did you, that he had a son—and a wife? They died."

"That's…awful," Azure said. "But—"

"This isn't over yet," Amber urged. "I'll be in touch."

She had hardly replaced the receiver before the phone rang again. Marco said, "Are you all right? I have been trying to contact you all evening."

"I've been partying with friends." Not that he needed to know about her social life. Booze made her talkative. "Having a good time," she embellished, just so he wouldn't think she'd spent all day chewing her nails about him and his diabolical plan. Although she had.

"Bueno," he said. "That's good."

"What do you want?" she asked.

"I have told you what I want, Amber." His voice descended to a deep purr, and she remembered that puma and jaguars prowled parts of his ranch—his *hato.* "I cannot stay away from home very much longer."

"I hope," she said, "you've realised how impossible—"

"Nothing is impossible," he contradicted her, "if one desires it enough."

And if one had unlimited money and power, she thought. "I talked to Azure," she reluctantly told him.

"Ah." A short pause. "What did she say?"

I'll do anything you want. You can't marry a man like

him. But Amber remembered how her sister's voice had wavered, the dejection and defeat in her tone.

Amber took a breath. "No test."

For a moment the line was silent. She couldn't even hear him breathing. Then, "So. Do you have a passport?"

"Yes." She swallowed hard.

"I filled in an application today for a marriage licence, which I am assured will be available in three days, and I am arranging a visa for you to enter Venezuela, which should be ready within a few more days, after you sign some forms and provide a birth certificate. We can be married, say, a week from today."

Feeling as though she'd just entered an alternate universe, she stammered, "You…you don't waste any time."

"As I said, I cannot spare too much of it."

"I'm willing to go to Venezuela with you, but I thought we'd be married there, after…well, after I've met your family and…got to know you better."

For a few seconds he said nothing, and she hoped he was considering the option.

But when he spoke he said, "You can meet them—and get to know me—after we are married. It is simpler to have the legal part taken care of here, so that you enter my country as my wife. Do not be concerned that I will insist on my rights against your wishes. We do, however, have things to discuss. May I visit you now?"

"I'm surprised you're asking my permission," she said. He never had before, since he'd barged into her life, turned it upside down and put her emotions into a constant merry-go-round.

"You are still angry with me," he said. "If it is not inconvenient I will be there in fifteen minutes."

* * *

"How can I tell my parents I'm marrying a man I've only just met and flying off to the other side of the world?" Standing in front of the fireplace in her sitting room, Amber spread her hands. *"Next week?"*

Marco hadn't sat down, either. He regarded her from a couple of metres away, his dark gaze steady and implacable. "We fell madly in love at first sight," he suggested. "We cannot wait to be together, and I am anxious to introduce my new bride to my own family."

"No! I won't do that. Anyway they'd never believe it."

"Then don't tell them we are getting married. Say you are to visit my home and we will come to know each other, as you suggested. Later we will tell them all they need to know."

"You're asking me to lie to them?"

He raised an ironic brow and she said defensively, "I never actually lied to you!"

"What you tell your family is up to you." Apparently losing interest. "I will book a time with the registrar. Do you have a preference? Morning, afternoon? Not too late. I would like to fly out the same day."

"I don't care." Her face suddenly felt cold and pinched, and Marco frowned, taking her arm. "You should sit down."

Amber shook his hand away. "I don't need to sit down. I can't believe you mean to go through with this."

"I do not easily change my mind." His voice lowered to a seductive tone. "I hope you will not change yours." He raised a hand and the back of one finger traced the line of her jaw to her chin, barely touching her skin.

Then he tipped her face, still with one finger, and kissed her so gently she felt her insides helplessly melting, before he drew her closer into his arms and kissed her more deeply, thoroughly. He took his time until she could bear it no longer and kissed him back, their mouths melding in an intimate slow dance.

When he drew away at last his hand pressed her head to his shoulder, and he kissed the tip of her ear, then her hair. Unbelievably she felt safe, not wanting to move out of Marco's warm embrace. He murmured, "It is not my intention to make you unhappy, *querida*."

She knew what that word meant—*darling*. Her heart did something weird, as though a tiny stiletto had pierced it. How could he do this to her so easily?

With an effort she stepped back.

It wasn't fair. His appalling proposition suddenly seemed not only possible but almost thrilling. The only time she'd felt remotely like this was when she was standing on a high bridge over a narrow river, seconds from her first and only bungee-jump. The same mixture of adrenaline, anticipation and sheer terror.

Then the terror had been mitigated by the knowledge that her ankles were comfortably secured to a strong, safety-tested rope.

This was like jumping without one.

She should tell Azure she couldn't go through with this after all, accept her sister's valiant offer to agree to the test. Then it would be all over. *If* Benny's DNA didn't match Marco's.

Instead she said through dry lips, "All right. Whenever you like. Now please leave me alone."

CHAPTER SIX

"But, *Amber*..." Azure's voice on the phone line conveyed her dismay. "I told you I'd—"

"I haven't married him yet." Prevarication. "I'm going to Venezuela to get to know him and his family. It's an interesting country and Marco's ranch—I guess you know it's called a *hato* over there—sounds fascinating. They have fantastic birdlife—parrots, flamingos, hundreds of others. I've been looking on the Internet." There was a lot more information on the wildlife than the custody laws.

The Salzano *hato* was mentioned on several travel blogs, and one site had a potted history of the family. On another she learned that Marco was a board member of an organisation dedicated to helping the native population dispossessed in past centuries by the Spanish invaders. Opening a large tract of Salzano land to small-farmers, he'd housed their families and built and staffed a school and medical clinic. It had made him unpopular with some other big landowners and even, it was hinted, members of his own family.

Azure said uncertainly, "You can't seriously be thinking of marrying him!"

Amber hesitated. "For Benny's sake. Yes."

"He'd be part of our family!" Panic filled Azure's voice. "What if—"

"Do you have a better idea?" Amber's tone sharpened in exasperation. "I don't want Benny caught in a custody fight any more than you do."

Then, contrite, she said, "It's okay. *I'm* okay. I've never done a proper OE like you and Rickie." Heading from their two-and-a-bit islands at the bottom of the Pacific for their "Overseas Experience" was for young Kiwis a rite of passage. "This is my chance. It'll be an adventure."

She told her parents she had the chance of working on an eco-heritage site in Venezuela, had to leave the following week and didn't know how long she'd be away. They weren't unused to her taking off at short notice, though previously she'd gone no farther than Australia—just across the "ditch," so-called, although the Tasman Sea was actually two thousand kilometres of notoriously rough water.

Skirting the truth was becoming a way of life for her. A distinctly uncomfortable thought.

When she gave a similar story to her studio boss, he was surprised and not pleased, but an assistant was happy to take over her job. She wondered about subleasing her flat, and decided keeping one option open gave her some sense of security, although possibly a spurious one. She'd ask Azure to keep an eye on the place.

The flight to Venezuela was long and exhausting, despite the unaccustomed, for Amber, comfort of first-class travel.

Too churned up to make small talk, she reflected with something close to panic that she didn't know her companion well enough for anything more personal.

She opened a Spanish/English phrase book, and now and then asked Marco to check her pronunciation. Sometimes she could see her effort amused him, but apart from crinkling about his eyes he kept a straight face. And occasionally he pointed out a difference between the standard Spanish in the book and Venezuelan variations.

When the cabin crew dimmed the lights she dozed while listening to a basic Spanish primer through an MP3 player, hoping the lessons would permeate her subconscious. But her mind kept going over the events of the past several days—lunch with her parents, dodging their questions with vague answers and keeping a smile on her face when she said goodbye. Then a farewell to her sister's family, evading Azure's efforts to get her alone and ignoring her worried eyes while chatting to Rickie and playing with the baby.

She gave Benny a last hug and he snuggled into her, stiffening her resolve. Then she hugged Azure again, whispering, "It's okay, Azzie. Everything's fine."

The wedding ceremony had been brief. It had rained and she'd been chilled in the pale-green dress and jacket that, after a great deal of mind-changing, she had hoped would be appropriate.

Marco had a carnation tucked into the buttonhole of his superbly well-fitted suit, and had handed her a small bouquet of sweet-scented freesias and cream rosebuds.

For some reason she choked up, wordlessly shaking her head as she took the flowers, then burying her face in them to hide her emotion. He'd taken her hand and kissed it, saying, "You are nervous, but it will soon be over."

Amber clamped her teeth then to stop a hysterical laugh.

Over? This was just the beginning.

* * *

After crossing the dateline and changing planes in Los Angeles and then Miami, by the time they landed at Simón Bolivar airport in Caracas Amber had no idea what the hour or even the day was back home.

Marco somehow had a car waiting for them with a driver who took them to a hotel in Caracas. She recalled that he had a place of his own in the city where he'd taken Azure. Perhaps he was being tactful. She looked longingly at the two beds in the room they were ushered into.

Marco said, "You need to rest properly before I introduce you to my family. Also, I have some business to conduct in the morning. I will make it as brief as possible, and I hope you will not mind being alone for a short while. Which bed would you like?"

So he didn't intend to share one, but right now she was too tired to feel anything. She dumped her shoulder bag on the closest one and said, "Do you want the bathroom?"

"We have two." Indicating the nearest of two doors.

Amber showered, and left the bathroom wearing a synthetic satin nightshirt. By the time Marco emerged from the other bathroom she was in bed and drifting into sleep.

She woke to full daylight and saw him standing before the window, dressed in a white shirt and casual sand-coloured trousers. When she sat up he must have heard the rustle of the sheets, and turned. "Good morning," he greeted her. "Do you feel better?"

"What time is it?" she asked. "What *day* is it?"

"Eleven o'clock," he answered. "And it is Wednesday."

Still? They'd left on Wednesday. Crossing the dateline had gained them an extra day.

She ran a hand over her sleep-tumbled hair. "You should have woken me."

"As I said, I had business in Caracas, and you looked much too…blissful to be woken. You sleep like an angel."

Disconcerted that he'd been studying her while she slept, Amber said, "You've been out already?"

"Yes. Now I am yours for the rest of the day."

Hers? She was very sure Marco Salzano was his own man and no-one else's. On the other hand, she was his—bought and paid for—until further notice.

She threw back the covers, not missing the interested study he made of her legs as she swung her feet to the floor and the nightshirt slid up. Quickly she stood, and after grabbing some undies and clothes from her suitcase made for the bathroom again.

When she came out Marco was lying on the other bed, his hands behind his head. He watched her replace her things in the suitcase and take out a brush and hair tie. She could see him in the mirror as she brushed out her hair into a ponytail and twisted the tie around to hold it. She'd put on fawn cotton trousers and a sleeveless shirt patterned with forget-me-nots. Air-conditioning cooled the room but she suspected that outside it would be hot.

Marco said, "If you wish we can stay here for another day or two. I will show you our capital city."

Amber put away the brush without facing him. "I thought you were in a hurry to get home."

"Yes," he conceded, getting off the bed, so that he was by her side when she turned from the suitcase. His hands went to her waist, lightly holding her, and quickening her blood. "But I'm aware that you find our…circumstances difficult. At the moment you look like a doe facing a hungry puma. A little time together before returning to Hato El Paraíso may help you to adjust."

Amber wasn't thrilled at the analogy comparing her to

a helpless animal, and had no particular wish to explore the city where he'd met her sister. Thinking about that made her voice cold, her words sharp. "A tour of Caracas won't help me adjust to being coerced into marrying you."

For an instant his hands tightened on her waist. Then he dropped them, stepping back, and said equally coolly, "Very well. I have some phone calls to make. Then we will eat lunch and this afternoon we will be home."

Over lunch the mood was strained. Marco's phone calls had been made in Spanish, and he had not told her what they were about. She let him order for her from the extensive, confusing menu, and he chose *empanada de pollo,* a sort of deep-fried turnover stuffed with chicken, saying it was a local dish he thought she would enjoy. She found it was a treat after airline food.

"Are your family expecting us—me?" she asked him. "Have you told them? Who actually lives at your... hacienda?" She was growing increasingly nervous, wondering what on earth his relatives would think of him bringing an unknown woman from the other side of the world home as his wife.

"My mother, my younger sister Ana Maria, my cousin Elena who organises the tourist part of our business and helps with the visitors. Another cousin, Diego, acts as a guide also. He has a degree in zoology, very helpful when scientists and ecologists come to the *hato.*"

"Your father...?" Amber asked tentatively.

"My father died some years ago," Marco said. "I spoke to my mother this morning. She will have informed my other sister that I am bringing home my bride. Paloma is married and has two delightful daughters. It would not surprise me if Paloma brings them and her husband to Hato El Paraíso as soon as she hears the news. She lives in Barinhas, our closest city. They will all want to meet you." He paused. "You will, *por favor,* not complain about your new husband to them. They are not to blame for my actions."

"Do you think I'd want to tell anyone I was forced to marry you?"

He said quietly, "I used no force. The choice was yours."

"Some choice!" She flashed him a hostile glance. "Between the devil and the deep blue sea."

"And I am the devil?" He gave her a sardonic look.

Amber remembered thinking when he first stormed into her life that he looked like Lucifer, the beautiful, arrogant angel so filled with pride he had challenged God Himself.

She shook her head. "You're only a man," she reminded him, and he laughed.

"That is true," he said, giving her a lazy, amused once-over that held appreciation. "And you, *querida,* are a woman. My wife."

He sounded so self-satisfied she flared again. "I may be your wife—legally—but I'm not your darling! This whole thing is a farce."

A brief shadow seemed to cross his aristocratic features. "I understand your resentment—" he said.

"Then why are you—"

Marco overrode her. "—But you will please curb it in front of my family. Or anyone else." Despite the phrasing, it was undoubtedly an order. "To the rest of the world we are passionately in love."

"That's difficult to fake."

"You are good at pretence."

She flushed, and he placed a hand over hers on the table. "I will make it as easy for you as I can," he said. "Let us take one day at a time, hmm?" He lifted her hand and kissed it, sending a reluctant shiver of warmth through her, and smiled a little crookedly before releasing her.

When Marco turned coaxing this way he was hard to resist. She wished her stupid heart would behave itself instead of going mushy, and reminded herself how ruthless he was at getting his way.

They took another flight to Barinhas, and after leaving the city she saw distant snow-capped mountains, some towns and tiny settlements. Thick vegetation covered the lower mountain slopes and smaller hillocks, and Amber was surprised to see palm trees waving their distinctive fronds above the other trees. Marco pointed out places of interest on the changing panorama far below.

After landing again they were driven to a remote corner of the airport, where a twin-engine plane waited outside a hangar.

She saw the logo of a leaping jaguar on the side, its lean, golden hide spotted with black rosettes, the muscular body at full stretch and sharp teeth painted brilliantly white. Beneath it were the words "Hato El Paraíso."

"You have your own plane?" she blurted out.

He said matter-of-factly, "It is useful for transporting our guests. And sometimes we need to get from place to place quickly, even on our own land. We also keep a helicopter."

Marco piloted the small plane himself, flying over a vast, flat plain of grassland changing from blue-green to straw-coloured, studded with occasional trees, and here and there browsed by huge, scattered herds of cattle whose pale hides merged into the grass. Muddy rivers snaked across the landscape through stands of junglelike trees and shrubs along their banks.

Eventually the aircraft glided in over what appeared to

be a village dominated by a large, U-shaped, tile-roofed building, before landing on a concrete airstrip several hundred metres away.

As Marco helped Amber out into warm, dry air, a truck took off from one of the outbuildings near the hacienda and, leaving a cloud of dust behind it, sped across the ground to come to a halt only a few metres from them.

A brown-skinned man with a crinkled face under a battered cowboy-style hat jumped from the driver's seat, directing a burst of rapid Spanish at Marco, who introduced the man as José.

José gave Amber two jerky little bows, and began enthusiastically unloading the luggage—mostly Amber's—and stacking it on the truck.

Amber and Marco climbed into the cab beside him and within minutes they arrived at the big house. An impressive colonnaded portico shaded wide steps leading up to a tiled terrace and a heavy, carved, open door, brass-studded and set into a whitewashed wall.

Two women appeared, one middle-aged with greying dark hair pinned in an elegant chignon, expertly applied make-up accentuating deep-set brown eyes and a full mouth. The other was young and also beautifully made up, with long curls arranged to look casual, like the perfectly fitted jeans she wore with a scarlet knit top.

"Buenas tardes, Madre," Marco said to the older woman, his hand on Amber's waist guiding her forward.

She said carefully, *"Buenas tardes, Señora Salzano."*

His mother's smile seemed strained as she greeted Amber with a kiss on her cheek.

Introduced to Marco's younger sister, Amber didn't miss the rather concentrated stare Ana Maria had given her, but the girl smiled when Amber held out her hand in greeting.

"You speak Spanish?" Ana Maria asked in English.

"I'm afraid not much," Amber confessed. "But I've been practising the basics. I will have to learn more."

Marco said, "You can help her, Ana Maria, and perhaps improve your English at the same time."

They moved inside and Amber was struck by how cool and dark it was. As her eyes adjusted she saw a wide passageway, its high ceiling supported by dark beams. An antique hall table with sturdy carved legs held a telephone and a bulbous terracotta bowl of flowers.

José was already on his way upstairs with several bits of luggage after consulting Señora Salzano, and Marco, his laptop slung over his shoulder and hers in his hand, led Amber the same way, saying they would rejoin his mother and sister in a few minutes. The room he took her to was spacious and featured an enormous carved bedstead covered with an elaborately embroidered spread and heaped with satin pillows in shades of red and gold.

All the furniture looked old, though lovingly polished, and the floor was dressed with a large woven rug. Two long, screened windows let in light and air, a breeze stirring the heavy curtains at the sides.

As José put down the cases and bags and quickly left, Amber skirted the bed, trying not to look at it, and went to stand at a window overlooking a courtyard surrounded by potted flowering plants. Beyond that a blue-tiled swimming pool shimmered in the afternoon sun.

"Do you want the bathroom?" Marco asked, indicating a door she hadn't even noticed.

"Later," she said.

He nodded, took a shirt from one of two huge freestanding wardrobes and entered the bathroom. The walls must be a foot thick, she thought, noting the depth of the door and window recesses.

When Marco emerged she scooted by him with an armful of clean clothing, make-up and toiletries. There was nothing wrong with what she had on, but the fresh-from-the-beauty-parlour appearance of the two Venezuelan women had made her feel like a country mouse.

When she emerged more than a few minutes later Marco gave an approving look at her jade-green silk shirt and bronze-coloured skirt worn with high-heeled gold sandals, taking in her smoothly brushed hair and re-done make-up.

Downstairs they found his mother and sister in what appeared to be a family room. Another young woman, about Amber's own age, was introduced as Elena, a cousin.

Not a hair was out of place in her smoothly combed-back coiffure, intricately plaited and pinned at the back. Bright lipstick highlighted her pretty mouth and flawless skin. A white blouse and wine-coloured skirt showed off an hourglass figure, the slim waist emphasised by a broad tooled-leather belt with an ornate brass buckle.

She gave Amber a cool smile before turning to Marco and speaking to him in rapid Spanish.

He said, "We will speak English, Elena. Amber does not know Spanish."

Elena's finely shaped brows rose. "*¿Qué?* None at all?"

"A few words," Amber said. "But I hope to learn it."

"I speak French, English, German and some Japanese," Elena told her. "As well as Spanish, of course."

Amber wasn't going to try competing with such a list of talents. She said, "You must be a great asset. Marco told me you organise the tourist business here."

"I help where I can." Elena looked cautiously pleased. "Marco is doing a wonderful job of protecting all the family's assets, even creating new ones. Although some of the old uncles make it difficult."

"Oh?" Amber was interested.

"They are stuck in the past, not understanding we must move with the times or lose our heritage." Elena gave a small laugh. "But of course you know nothing of the economics and politics of our country."

How could she be so sure? However, Amber was conscious that her knowledge was limited and not firsthand.

Marco took her arm and guided her to a wide cowhide sofa where he sat beside her.

A young woman introduced as Filipa brought in coffee on a tray, then left the room, and Señora Salzano poured for them. She asked Amber a few stilted questions in English, mostly about her family, but was obviously relieved to lapse into Spanish when addressing her son.

The room was large but comfortably furnished with deep chairs, convenient side tables, and a state-of-the-art entertainment centre complete with an enormous TV screen.

"You like television?" Ana Maria asked her, seeing her looking at it. "I love to watch the *telenovela*."

"English," Marco chided his sister. And to Amber, "She means soap opera. She and her girlfriends are all hooked on those silly stories. They like to cry over them."

Ana Maria protested, "You are a man! You cannot understand the emotions of women."

Suspecting that was true, Amber said, "Actually I like stories that deal with relationships." With a woman-to-woman smile at Ana Maria, she added, "Men do seem uncomfortable with them."

Marco gave her a piercing look and she wondered if the remark came under the ban on showing her family the real nature of their marriage, but he told his sister, "Amber worked in television."

Ana Maria's eyes widened, and even though she seemed a little disappointed when Amber explained she wasn't an actress but a behind-the-scenes worker, she was happy to chat on about TV, fashion and American film stars.

Later the other sister arrived as predicted, with her husband and children. Paloma had the same faultless appearance as Señora Salzano and Ana Maria.

The girls, aged seven and five—delectably attired in matching frilled dresses, their hair tied with ribbons—ran to their uncle Marco, who effortlessly lifted each of them high in the air before giving them a kiss and hug, and made them giggle with jokes in Spanish.

Amber shouldn't have been surprised. His longing for a child was the reason Marco had brought her here because he'd lost his own son. He was capable of loving children. And obviously fond of his sister and mother.

One day he might even be fond of her.

CHAPTER SEVEN

AT EIGHT o'clock Filipa, the maid, reappeared, and the whole family repaired to another big room where they sat down at a large table.

The meal was light and leisurely, with conversation in both English and Spanish. Everyone used their hands to illustrate a point—even Marco—although she hadn't noticed him doing so before. She guessed that he tempered his mannerisms to the company he was in. Trying to copy the local etiquette, she kept her hands above the table and when she was finished left a little food on her plate and placed her knife and fork sideways with handles on the tabletop like everyone else.

"Have you had enough to eat?" Marco asked her softly.

She nodded. "It was delicious."

He apparently relayed that in Spanish to his mother, and the *señora* smiled and nodded at her. No one seemed in a hurry to move, and Amber tried to hide a yawn. Embarrassed, she murmured, "Excuse me. It's been a long journey."

Marco gave a quiet laugh and pushed back his chair, saying, "I will take you up to our room." He spoke to his mother, then he pulled out Amber's chair for her to a chorus of understanding *"Buenas noches."*

Marco laid a hand on her waist as they ascended the stairs, and she wondered if he looked on this as their wedding night—the night she'd anticipated with very mixed emotions, encompassing dread and rather mortifying expectation and a whole lot in between.

A sturdy, grey-haired woman wearing a black dress was coming down the stairs, and Marco stopped to kiss her cheek and introduce her to Amber. "Concepcion has cared for the whole family," he said, "since my sisters and I were children. We could not do without her." He said something in Spanish to her, perhaps a translation, and she laughed and lightly slapped his arm before turning a bright, beady stare filled with curiosity on Amber. After a moment she gave a small nod and burst into a torrent of Spanish.

"What did she say?" Amber asked as she and Marco continued on their way.

"Too much," he answered. A glance at his face showed her an unsmiling, rather forbidding expression. But his voice changed to a lighter note and he said, "She wishes us well, and that you will give me many healthy children."

He opened the door of the room and switched on a light. "I will leave you to get yourself to bed," he said. "In an hour or so I will be back."

Did he expect her to wait for him? So they could consummate their bizarre marriage?

She stood indecisively where she was, and he touched her cheek with an index finger. "You are still tired," he said. "I will not disturb your sleep. Do you need anything?"

She said no, and he withdrew, closing the door.

The bedclothes had been turned down, her gold satin pyjamas laid across the left side of the bed, and the magnificent cover neatly folded on the box at its foot. Her luggage had gone, and when she opened a wardrobe she found her skirts and trousers and dresses hanging there. Her hairbrush and make-up were arranged on the dressing table.

She found her toiletries in the bathroom, alongside unused soaps, bath oils and bottles of bubble bath she'd noticed earlier. A fresh fluffy towel had replaced the one she'd hung on the brass rail after her shower.

Ten minutes later she slid into the big bed between crisp linen sheets and switched off the bedside light. Another glowed at the far side of the bed, and she turned her back to it.

Images of the past couple of days drifted across her closed eyelids: the various planes with their droning engines; the changing views from her window seats, which Marco had insisted she take; the seemingly arbitrary way night changed to day and then night again; and above all Marco, the volatile, determined, sexy and scary stranger to whom she was, unbelievably, married.

She woke to the sound of birds screeching and twittering. A chink between drawn curtains at the window showed a glimmer of light, and she could faintly hear the shower running.

Quickly she looked at the other half of the bed and dimly saw the sheet flung back in a heap, the pillow dented. Marco had slept there and she'd never even known.

Curious about this place that was his home, she left the bed and parted the curtains further. Daylight was turning the sky grey, edged with pale, luminous pink, and a tiny bird hovered at the window, its wings an almost invisible whirr of movement. She'd never seen a hummingbird before, and watched with fascination until it flew off and disappeared into a nearby tree.

Other birds were distantly silhouetted against the sky, soaring alone or erupting in dense flocks, and a group of multi-coloured parrots streaked across her vision as the bathroom door opened. She turned and Marco emerged, a towel slung about his hips, his hair damp and uncombed. He looked perfectly at ease and very sexy. She couldn't help appreciating his strong, muscular body.

"Ah," he said. *"Buenos días."* His gaze took in the enveloping pyjamas, a hint of amusement in his eyes when they met hers again, and he came towards her.

Her body tensed and something fluttered in her throat. Marco halted, his eyes narrowing. "Don't look at me so."

"I don't know what you mean."

"As if you expect me to leap on you like some wild beast."

He turned away to stride to a massive chest of drawers and after dropping the towel pulled on underpants that fitted taut over his lean flanks, then jeans and a white tee.

"I have work to do," he said tersely, picking up a comb without looking at her. Dragging it through his hair, he said, "I will ask Filipa to bring you breakfast. What time would you like it?"

"I'd rather have my breakfast when everyone else does."

"Later, then. Eight o'clock. I thought you would sleep longer. This morning I must join the *llaneros.* I will try to be here for lunch. Go back to bed."

"I'm awake now," she said. "I might go for a walk, explore a bit."

"Not alone." He put the comb down and faced her. "Ana Maria may take you out. Or I will myself, later. I regret I must leave you now, but some problems have arisen while I was away."

She breakfasted a couple of hours later with his mother, sister and cousin, the table offering pineapple slices, scrambled eggs with corn patties called *arepas,* and cheeses, rolls and jam with iced fruit juice and coffee.

Afterwards Ana Maria took her on a tour of the house, its airy rooms cooled by large ceiling fans, the tiled bathrooms modernised by up-to-date plumbing and fittings.

One wing was for visitors, the rooms furnished simply but with comfortable beds and adjoining bathrooms. "We get a lot of bird-watchers and naturalists," Ana Maria said. "And backpackers, from all over the world."

The kitchen area, presided over by a small woman with a big smile, was vast. A long, scrubbed wooden table stood at its centre, and a huge old wood stove vied with a gleaming stainless steel electric cooker and oven, a huge dishwasher and two large fridge/freezers.

In the living rooms the heavy, dark furniture wasn't crowded together, nor cluttered by too many ornaments, adding to the cool, spacious look of the rooms. Pictures and woven rugs decorated the white walls.

Marco's office was on the ground floor. When Ana Maria knocked and opened the door, Elena looked up from a computer set on one of two large desks, asking rather abruptly, "What do you want, Ana?"

Amber said hastily, "Let's not disturb Elena."

"What else would you like to see?" Ana Maria asked.

"Is it dangerous to take a walk on my own, if I don't go too far?" It shouldn't be difficult in the flat landscape to keep the hacienda in sight. Amber hadn't forgotten Marco's warning, but his assumption she would obey his injunction not to walk alone rankled a little.

Ana Maria shrugged. "The big cats don't come near inhabited areas, usually. But it is not very interesting. If you want to see animals and birds I will show you."

"I don't want to take you from your studies."

"No problema. I can study another time. You will need a wide hat," Ana Maria advised, "to protect your complexion. I will lend you one of mine."

In a well-used, four-wheel-drive vehicle, they drove along a dusty unsealed road leading away from the hacienda. Amber saw a large brown form ahead, like a big fat dog sitting on the road, but as they drew closer it more nearly resembled a giant guinea pig. "Is that a capybara?" she asked.

"You know of them?" Ana Maria seemed surprised.

"From the Internet. The largest rodent on earth?"

"Sí." Ana Maria stopped so they could get out and, after allowing Amber to photograph it, nudged the apparently sleeping animal aside. It huffed grumpily off on its short legs and settled in the grass beside the road.

It wasn't the last they saw, nor the last that had to be moved, after they began crossing the grass on narrow roads built several feet higher than the surrounding land.

"To trap some of the water after the wet season," Ana Maria explained, "so it doesn't dry up completely."

"Do you help guide the tourists?" Amber asked her.

"Sometimes, when I'm home. I am studying social science at university," she said, "but now I am between semesters."

A little later she told Amber, "Marco has been terribly secretive about you. We didn't even know he had a sweetheart until he telephoned and said he was bringing home his bride! It is so romantic! Did he really go all the way to New Zealand to ask you to marry him?"

"Something like that." Amber tried to smile. "What *did* he tell you?" They had better synchronise their stories.

"Only that he had met a New Zealand woman some time ago and had not forgotten her. She—you wrote to him, and I guess he wrote back. Or e-mailed. Love letters?" Curiosity and mischief danced in Ana Maria's dark eyes. "From my brother?" As if she found it difficult to imagine.

"Not exactly," Amber murmured.

Fortunately Ana Maria didn't demand any elaboration. "And you too were unable to forget."

Amber supposed she should make some comment. "Marco's not easily forgotten."

"He said you were beautiful and clever."

Clever? That could be a double-edged word. As for beautiful, perhaps there was novelty value in being fair-skinned and fair-haired where most people were darker.

"And," Ana Maria continued, "he had to marry you quickly so he could bring you back with him in case you changed your mind. But you wouldn't have, would you? You are in love with my brother, *sí?*"

"Why else would I have married him?" Amber made her voice light, erasing all trace of irony.

"Of course our mother would like a proper church wedding. But Marco said wait until you have settled, got used to us all. *Mi Madre* tried to insist, but Marco…once he makes up his mind—" Ana Maria shrugged "—he is like a rock. You can push and push but get nowhere."

Tell me about it. Amber forced a smile.

Eventually they left the road to go cross-country, where tracks in the tall grass showed other vehicles had taken the same route to a riverside where capybaras swam with frogs and turtles, and butterflies floated like confetti through the trees. But most ubiquitous of all were the birds—parrots of all colours, wading birds and swimming birds, geese bending the branches of trees, storks and wrens, vultures, birds Amber had never seen nor imagined. She had used up all the storage on her video and still cameras by the time Ana Maria said it was time to leave.

Lunch was served to the women at two o'clock in the dining room. Filipa brought cool fruit drinks and a beef and rice dish, followed by a fruit dessert. Marco arrived late, going upstairs to change before joining them.

Afterwards Señora Salzano went to her room to rest. Elena disappeared too and Ana Maria took what looked like a textbook to the back of the hacienda, where a wide shaded terrace bordering the courtyard held chairs and small tables, and a couple of loungers.

Alone with Amber, Marco asked, "Can you ride a horse?"

"For a while my sister and I belonged to a pony club."

"I will take you riding when it is cooler and more animals are likely to be about. Now you should rest."

"Is that what you do in the afternoon?"

"Often I do paperwork, although much of it is done on a computer, not paper. My study is cool. But if you wish we can have a siesta together." A gleam entered his eyes, and hers shied from it.

"I'm not used to the idea of a siesta," she said. "I'd rather swim, if that's all right. I'm sure you have a lot to attend to after being away."

"As you say. Elena has left me a pile of correspondence." He turned towards his study, and Amber went upstairs for her swimsuit and a towel.

The pool was enclosed by a high, white-painted wall with a wooden gate. At one end of the enclosure a tile-roofed, open structure sheltered a barbecue and several chairs and tables, and sun-loungers were placed on the wide surround.

The water looked invitingly cool and sparkling clean, and after the first shock on diving in and a few laps of Australian crawl, Amber turned on her back and floated.

A flock of multicoloured birds passed across her vision, and she watched them out of sight. The sound of the gate clicking drew her attention, and she flurried upright as Marco, wearing bottle-green swim shorts that revealed rather than concealed his masculinity, discarded the towel slung over his shoulder and took a long, shallow dive, coming up less than a metre from her.

Water streamed from his flattened hair, which he shoved back with his fingers as he stood waist deep. His teeth gleamed white in a smile, and she could see herself in miniature, reflected in his dark, glowing eyes.

"I thought you were working," she said.

"It was hard to concentrate." He didn't touch her but she felt his gaze like a lingering touch as it encompassed her, taking note of the low cut of her flower-patterned bathing suit, and the way it clung to her breasts, waist and hips and was cut high at the thigh. "I thought of my new bride alone in the pool. It did not seem right."

She had thought the suit rather modest, falling for its splashy hibiscus flowers in hot-pink, orange and yellow against a blue background, and had chosen it instead of a bikini last summer. Yet she had never felt as naked as she did now, with Marco's eyes lit by the unmistakable flame of desire, and his much more nearly nude, magnificent body within touching distance.

He looked as though he'd like to devour her. Momentarily she recalled the white-painted teeth of the jaguar on the side of his plane, and a small shiver passed over her.

"You are cold?" he said.

"No." The water felt quite warm now. But her voice sounded thin, wary.

His smile vanished. "I will not rape you, Amber."

He'd seen her flash of alarm and correctly interpreted it. Chagrined that she'd shown panic, she said, "You have no need to, do you? You know you've got me over a barrel."

Marco cocked his head. "A barrel? The picture is—" He raised a dark eyebrow and broke off, shaking his head. "I don't know the expression."

"It means, I will have to sleep with you because you won't let me go until I have your baby."

His mouth compressed and she saw his jaw go tight. "It is what you agreed to," he acknowledged. "Are you contemplating breaking our bargain?"

"No. Unless you've thought better of it."

"That is not an option," he warned harshly. "We will not speak of it again." He turned and began swimming with long, somehow angry strokes to the deep end of the pool.

Amber lifted her feet and swam to the other end. She reached the short ladder and was climbing out when a hand closed around her ankle.

Marco said, "Come, it is too soon to leave. You have hardly begun to cool off."

"I'm cool enough."

He released her ankle, but before she could move he had his hands at her waist, hauling her back into the water.

Consumed by the anger that had been simmering below the surface since he'd first suggested she marry him, Amber tried to kick backwards, but the water made it a feeble effort and she heard Marco's low laughter, his breath at her ear. His arms went about her waist and her fury increased. She squirmed, turning to beat at him with her fists, thudding against his chest, his face, anywhere she could reach, until he drew in a hissing breath and she knew with a mixture of triumph and horror that she'd succeeded in hurting him.

He dragged her wrists down with implacable hands and clipped them behind her, pulling her against him. She could tell he was aroused, but his eyes glittered with temper that made her heart jump in fright.

CHAPTER EIGHT

"You will not strike me," Marco said, his voice deep and quiet but laced with steely purpose, "ever again. I will not allow it. You understand?"

Amber stared into his eyes, determined not to drop her gaze and let him win, think he'd cowed her.

"I'm not a servant!" she said. "Or a child. You can't—" *give me orders.* But he didn't allow her to finish.

"Then do not act like a child," he said.

He had a point—she'd never hit anyone since she was ten and Azure only seven and a quarrel had turned physical. Both of them ended up crying—not so much because the marks of Azure's teeth were clearly visible on Amber's arm, and Amber had a handful of Azure's hair, but because they'd upset themselves by hurting each other. Now she felt a similar mixture of rage and misery. But she said, "Then don't you act like a Neanderthal! Is that how Venezuelan men treat their women?"

"I did not harm you," he argued. "Another man might have hit you back. I will never strike a woman."

"You *grabbed* me to force me to do what you wanted." She glared defiance, and perhaps it was surprise at her standing up to him that momentarily flickered in his eyes.

"I merely wished to suggest you stay a little longer. On my way here I passed Ana Maria and she knew you were already swimming. It would have looked odd if you left immediately after I joined you. I 'grabbed' you in play. At first I thought you too were playing." The grimness in his expression was replaced by a rueful curve of his mouth. "I was not aware I had married a little hellcat."

"I'm not!" Amber protested. "It's years since I lost my temper like that." She shifted but he still held her. "I suppose," she admitted, "I overreacted. Sorry I hurt you."

"*De nada.* It was nothing." He paused, then said rather stiffly, "I also am sorry if I upset you."

Amber gave a jerky nod of acknowledgement. He'd apologised, and she didn't carry grudges.

"I think," Marco said thoughtfully, "that I may have a bruise...right here." Touching the skin just below his lower lip, he added lightly, "You could perhaps kiss it better, hmm?"

Amber went very still. There were a bare couple of centimetres between them, and she felt the heat of his body despite the cool water lapping about them.

"Is that not what you do after a quarrel?" he asked, scarcely above a whisper. "Kiss and make up?"

Somehow his words, and his almost nude body, so tantalisingly close to hers with its flimsy, wet Lycra covering, created a potent, sensual aura that she couldn't—didn't want to—resist.

This man was her husband, unlikely though that had seemed only days ago. She had promised to give him her body, make love with him—or at least have sex.

"Well?" he queried softly, and she realised he was waiting for her to make the first move, trying to demonstrate to her that he wouldn't coerce it.

Sometime she had to accept that this was why she

was here, that he had a right to ask her to fulfil her part of the devil's deal they'd made. She should be grateful for his patience.

She tilted her head up, tiptoed and put her lips to the place he'd indicated, for the whole of one second. She smelled the scent of his skin, felt the slight roughness where he'd shaved. Her upper lip touched his lower one.

Amber hesitated, and then he shifted fractionally so that her mouth met his. Her breasts brushed against his chest, immediately reacting, and she knew he must feel it.

Marco's arms brought her closer again, his mouth taking over her tentative kiss, parting her lips to a passionate but controlled exploration, teasing and tantalising, inviting and demanding, gentle and yet passionate.

His hands roved over her back, bared by the bathing suit, and slid to her behind, then cupped her and lifted her to him, and her heart rate accelerated into a fast drumbeat. Her body was suffused by fire. She had her arms about his neck, and his hands went to her thighs, lifting her even further so that she instinctively wrapped her legs about him and felt the hardness of him at the apex where the myriad, unimaginable sensations that thrilled through her being had their centre.

But suddenly Marco was pushing her away, pulling her arms down, and her legs slid from him, her feet finding the bottom of the pool. His face was dark, his eyes brilliant, and his jawline like granite.

"Not here," he said grittily. "Not our first time. That should be…in a more appropriate place. A private place, where I can make love to you properly. When I make you truly my wife it will be our real wedding night, slow and sweet and memorable, not a hurried coupling where we could be discovered at any moment."

Of course he was right. What if Ana Maria had decided to join them? Or even Elena, perhaps, thinking she'd like to cool off after her morning's work?

"Go," Marco said, "before I lose my self-control completely." Then he turned and began ferociously swimming away from her, the water parting before his powerful arms.

Amber's legs wobbled as she clambered up the steps. She was shivering, but not with cold. She snatched up her towel, at first holding it to herself like a security blanket, her eyes tightly closed while water dripped from her hair and she tried to orientate herself, until her body returned to something like normal.

When she forced her eyes open everything seemed more sharply delineated than before. She was hyper-aware of the heat of the sun on her skin, the way its light caught the droplets of water that Marco splashed up, the dazzling white of the walls about the pool, the stillness of the trees that grew beyond them.

She fastened the towel firmly above her breasts, the centres still furled and tingling. Wrenching her thoughts away from how Marco's hard chest had felt against them, she wrung out her hair, took several deep breaths and walked towards the gate. She had no idea how long that torrid episode had taken—perhaps only minutes—but she needed to compose herself and get some clothes on before she could face her husband again.

Her husband. It felt strange, alien. Like the man himself.

Last night they had slept in the same bed, although she had been unaware of his presence beside her. He wouldn't wait forever for her to fulfil her marriage vows.

When Amber crossed the courtyard Ana Maria didn't look up from her book, and she met no one on the way to the bedroom. She lost no time in drying herself properly and slipping into fresh undies and a loose cotton dress. She used the dryer in the bathroom on her hair until it was only slightly damp, and fastened it back with a tie.

When she emerged Marco was in the bedroom, wearing jeans, zipped but not fastened, and he was pulling a T-shirt over his head, his damp towel crumpled on the floor.

Averting her eyes from the tantalising glimpse of a rather magnificent male form, Amber walked to her dressing table and began fiddling with the things on its top. Her minimal make-up gone and her hair pulled back from her face, she looked naked—pale and washed-out compared with the warm skin tones of the Venezuelan women, enhanced by their impeccable make-up, drawing attention to dark-lashed eyes and luscious lips. The Internet had told her Venezuelans had won world beauty contests more often than those from any other country.

How could she compete?

Men had sometimes called her beautiful, but she'd always taken it with a grain of salt. She had no doubt that the woman she thought of as Marco's wife—his *real* wife—would have been a genuine beauty. He wouldn't have settled for anything less. Probably from a wealthy and respected old family like his own, she'd have had all the qualities required of a Salzano bride, cultured and knowledgeable about the customs and mores of her class, she wouldn't have been always on the alert in case she inadvertently broke some unspoken rule of conduct.

She'd have been able to speak freely with Señora Salzano in their own language, perhaps viewed soap operas with Ana Maria. And she had given Marco a son. The son he'd adored.

Marco had loved her.

Suddenly Amber was silently crying, hot tears spilling

down her cheeks. She saw them in the mirror and shut her eyes in a futile attempt to stop them.

Two hands descended on her shoulders, turning her. Marco said, "There is no need for tears."

Amber tried to pull away from him, scrubbing at her wet cheeks, her voice rising. "I've been bullied into marriage with a man I scarcely know, dragged I don't know how many thousands of miles from my home, family, friends, a job I loved, and from my own country—where I could walk in the bush without worrying I might be savaged by some wild animal—to a strange place in the back of beyond where I can't even speak the language. And you tell me not to cry! Well, *stuff you,* I'll cry a damned river if I want to!"

She sniffed, swiped a hand across her eyes where the tears had miraculously stopped, and said with irritated passion, "Only, I *hate* tears!" They were Azure's specialty. Amber was the strong one. "And don't you *dare* laugh at me!"

Because although he'd listened gravely enough to her list of grievances, perhaps even with some sympathy in his eyes—guilt was too much to read there, surely—at her final outburst Marco's mouth had twitched at the corners, and the skin at the corners of his eyes was crinkling.

He controlled his expression and said, "I beg your pardon, *querida,*" sounding so sincere she eyed him with deep suspicion.

She scowled, and muttered without conviction, "I told you not to call me that."

His mouth was firmly closed and perfectly straight, but the amusement in his eyes hadn't completely disappeared.

"I regret," he said, "that I could not give you more time to become accustomed to the idea of marrying me. There are matters here that require my attention. Naturally you will miss your home for a time. Tomorrow you must speak with your parents, perhaps your sister."

"Is that an order?"

He seemed puzzled, not answering immediately. "It is a suggestion. One I thought you would welcome."

"It's just," she said crossly, "you have a habit of expressing yourself in commands. Like telling me not to go walking alone."

"You could become lost, or come across something unexpected. An anaconda. Or a caiman. Even a rattlesnake."

Amber scarcely contained a shudder, the standard reaction of a Kiwi to snakes and alligators or crocodiles. Ana Maria had shown her several small crocodile-like caimans, but meeting a bigger one alone would have freaked her.

Marco shifted his hands to cup her face, wiping at the residue of tears with his thumbs. "In a couple of hours I will take you to meet some of these dangerous creatures, and will make sure you come to no harm." He patted her cheek and dropped his hands. "I will see you later."

When the door closed behind him, Amber drooped, suddenly too tired even to rouse annoyance at his patronising manner. The wide bed under the silently whirling ceiling fan looked overwhelmingly inviting.

She kicked off the sandals she'd donned and lifted the cover away, then lay down and reached for her book on the bedside table. But she had read only a few pages before her eyelids fell and she let the book drop to her chest.

Marco stared at the spreadsheet on the screen in front of him. The figures before him refused to make sense.

He kept thinking of Amber—the way her body had felt against his in the pool, how she'd kissed him, with that brief, shy touch of her lips. Then, when he held her closer, she'd opened her mouth to his persuasion and he'd felt the soft mounds of her breasts pressing against him, the tiny hardened peaks that told him she wanted him. That knowledge had increased his own desire, and he'd had to battle for some semblance of control.

When her lovely legs wound about him he'd almost lost it, wanting to tear away the thin barriers of cloth between them and plunge himself into her there and then.

Fortunately, sanity had stepped in just in time. Had he not already taken too much from this woman, driven by his own needs, his wants? He could at least choose a more suitable venue to first slake his growing lust for her.

As she'd just reminded him, he'd torn her from everything—everyone—she knew and brought her to the other side of the world, to a place where she knew nothing and no one. What had she called it—the back of beyond?

He smiled. Even in tears she had delivered him a diatribe, a catalogue of his sins. Which were many, as no one knew so well as he.

And this latest was the blackest of all, as conscience and reason and his father's training in honour, the mark of a true *hidalgo*, a noble man, constantly reminded him. Yet he would not give up. Could not. Fate had presented him with this one chance to fulfil his heart's desire.

When the idea had first entered his mind he knew it was reprehensible, iniquitous. His mother and his dead father would have condemned it. He might have dismissed it out of hand, except for one thing: no matter how much she protested, how often she spat words at him like a cornered she-cat, Amber responded to him sexually. The inexplicable pull of attraction—that wayward, God-given and seemingly arbitrary compulsion between a man and a woman—

had grown stronger each time they met, regardless of her efforts to hide it, fight it, pretend it didn't exist.

His disappointment when he'd thought no baby existed had been much more painful than he would have anticipated, biting sharp and deep. Correspondingly, his anger at Azure's refusal to confirm whether the child was his had seared his soul. Even though he had come reluctantly to admire Amber's steadfast defence of her family, his inability to control his desire for her also angered him.

In the end, every other way to a solution proved unworkable. So he'd stifled the grumblings of conscience and heritage, sure that Amber would in time come willingly to his bed. And then...

Then he would get what he wanted, as he almost invariably did. And no one would be hurt.

His absent stare wandered from the computer screen to a framed photograph on top of a filing cabinet. A dark-haired woman holding a little boy smiled back at him.

He let out a sharp breath, went to the cabinet and picked up the photo. Frowning down at it, he ran a thumb over the picture, then opened the top file drawer and dropped the photo at the very back before pushing the drawer shut with a thud.

Amber woke at the soft opening and closing of the bedroom door. She'd fallen first into a light doze, semi-aware of the twittering of birds outside that contrasted with the stillness of the house, while images floated through her mind—her family, Benny's endearing chuckle, Azure's distraught face when she heard that Marco was in New Zealand, and Marco himself in his many moods from fury to cold implacability to unexpected gentleness.

Before sleep overcame her she'd almost imagined

herself back home in her own bed, but on opening her eyes she saw the fan circling above her, the high beamed ceiling, and then Marco coming towards her.

She sat up so quickly that for a second she was dizzy. Her hair was dry now, but she checked the pillow behind her with her palm.

"What is it?" Marco inquired.

"I'm afraid I've left a damp patch on the pillow." She hadn't put a towel down. "My hair…"

Marco shrugged. "Concepcion will bring a new one."

How nice to take things like that for granted, Amber thought acidly. To know that if you spoiled something it would be fixed for you, that if you made a mess someone else would clean it up.

Her female friends joked that they could do with a wife, but here a wife wasn't expected to do daily chores. Not if she was married to a Salzano. All Marco required of her was sex and a baby, the former being nothing but a means to an end. If she lay back and thought of England—or of the Salzano empire—he'd be satisfied.

"Did you sleep?" he asked. "Are you ready to go out?"

Sleeping in the daytime made her muzzy. She swung her feet to the ground. "I can do with some fresh air. Give me five minutes while I change."

Marco nodded and turned to look out of the window, for which she was grateful. In the bathroom she spread sunscreen over her face and hands and put on light cotton trousers and a buttoned shirt. Back in the bedroom, surveying the row of shoes stowed on the floor of the wardrobe, she asked Marco, "Will sneakers be all right?"

He turned. "If you have no suitable boots."

His boots had heels, which made him seem even taller when she'd laced her sneakers and he came towards her again. "You may need a jacket," he said. "And bring your video camera."

She picked up the camera, from which she had downloaded her morning's work onto her computer, ready for more filming. "You don't mind?" she queried him.

He shrugged. "You did not buy it for nothing."

He had watched her choose the camera at the duty-free store, apparently intrigued by the fact she knew exactly what she wanted in her purchase and how to find it.

Outside, a short way from the house, a dozen or so horses were corralled in a large enclosure. Two were tied to the railing, already saddled.

"This is Domitila." Marco patted the neck of a dappled grey mare with powerful shoulders and graceful legs who snorted and turned her head to nuzzle at his shoulder. "Come and meet her." He petted the mare's straight, short head, and the pointed ears flicked in greeting.

Her alert eyes turned to Amber as Marco stepped back.

"She's lovely," Amber said, caressing the velvety nose.

"She is a direct descendant of the conquistador horses who were left to run wild. Our feral horses are small but very strong and hardy. Crossbreeding with Thoroughbreds from Europe and North America produced a unique strain suited to our land. Domitila has no vices. You will be safe."

He untied the reins, and Amber refused his help to mount, but let him tighten the girth and adjust her stirrups.

Marco vaulted easily onto the other horse, a dark bay with a black mane and tail, who tossed his head and danced a bit before Marco urged him forward, along the drive and then onto an unsealed road.

"You have seen capybaras today?" Marco asked as they came upon a family of them making their slow way to a pond.

"Yes. They're amazingly tame."

"They are the fourth or fifth generation that has not been hunted or molested on the *hato*. Also," Marco added dryly, "they are very lazy. A biologist who came here to study their behaviour gave up after a few weeks of sitting around waiting for them to do something other than eat, sleep, and cool off in a pond or lagoon, where they also mate—reputedly up to twenty or thirty times a day when the mood takes them."

Amber laughed, and he grinned at her, making her stomach flip. She had never before seen him look as relaxed, and she felt a loosening of the tension that was always there between them. She raised her brows sceptically, wondering if he was pulling her leg, as her own compatriots sometimes did, teasing gullible tourists. She said, "No wonder they're tired."

Marco laughed. "They do no work," he pointed out.

They walked the horses a bit further while Amber became used to Domitila and let the horse get to know her. It was she who increased the pace when they left the hacienda environs with its corrals and outbuildings behind and headed along one of the road-cum-dykes.

In the distance she saw what looked like huge red poppies among the pale grasses, until one soared into the sky, followed by dozens of others.

"Scarlet ibis," Marco explained.

A scattered herd of cattle grazed knee-deep in the pale, coarse grass. Humpbacked, creamy animals sporting wide, lethal-looking curved horns, Amber thought they appeared underfed, with prominent bones and long, skinny legs, unlike the fat, sleek cattle she knew.

"They are bred to withstand the conditions in this country," Marco told her. "We have only two seasons, the dry and the wet. Before the rains begin these beasts will be sold or moved to better pasture for fattening."

In time they reached open forest, which became thicker as they approached a bend in the river that fed it. Tall palms pushed above other trees, and something dropping rapidly through the branches startled Amber and made Marco's horse shy and skitter backwards until his strong, capable hands brought it under control.

Amber's placid mare simply ignored the large rust-red monkey now hanging with one hand from a branch only a metre or so from them and regarding Amber with a quizzical expression that made her laugh.

The monkey grinned, and then swung away into the tangle of trees and creepers while the riders continued until they reached a wide stretch of water that Marco called a lagoon.

A flock of storks took off into the sky, and at the water's edge two long crocodile-like caimans basked, open mouths displaying rows of pointed teeth. As she pulled on the horse's reins they turned and, moving surprisingly quickly, slid into the murky water.

Marco halted his horse and dismounted to come to Amber's side as she swung to the ground. His hands went to her waist from behind, and into her ear he whispered, "Shh."

Silently he pointed to a huge rock near the edge of the lagoon, in its shadow something like a heap of smooth, muddied stone.

Her breath caught when she realised it was an enormous, coiled snake, and she involuntarily took a step back, coming up against Marco's lean, hard body. His hands tightened and she felt laughter shake his chest but he made no sound. "Anacondas are not poisonous, though they can bite. Do you want to film it?"

"It isn't moving," Amber pointed out. "That thing would hardly show up at all on film."

Marco left her and moved cautiously forward. When she

saw the snake's greenish-brown body ripple and it began to uncoil, Amber stifled an urge to scream. Then Marco lunged, and when he straightened he had a firm grip on the snake's head while its sinuous body twisted in protest, its pale pink mouth gaping.

Amber's hands shook as she focused the camera and started it running. Surely what Marco was doing was dangerous? The snake was as thick as his powerful thighs, and must be at least six metres long. Yet he held its writhing body as nonchalantly as if it were an animated toy, even when its tail end began to coil about him.

"That's enough," she told him in strangled tones.

"Do you want to touch it?" he asked.

Touch it? The last thing she wanted, but an unwilling fascination, mingled with misguided pride that made her not want to appear a wussy female in front of him, interfered with her sense of preservation and propelled her forward.

She put a hand gingerly on the snake's skin, surprised to find it warm and dry, the muscles beneath strongly flexing in its effort to escape.

The intricate, symmetrical design of its tiny scales, olive-green with gold spots, was beautiful, and she fancied that its small gleaming eye held a fear equal to her own.

Stepping back, she said, "Let it go."

When Marco did, she raised the camera again and filmed the anaconda slithering away, sliding its entire body with remarkable speed into the water.

"Did you get a good shot?" Marco asked.

"Yes. But you've no need to show off your machismo for me," Amber replied rather tightly. "I wouldn't have had a clue what to do if that thing had attacked you."

He laughed. "I have been doing this for tourists since I was a boy." Then he looked at her closely. "She was not big enough to harm me. The females can grow to three times that size. And I am not defenceless." He indicated a sheathed knife tucked into his belt. "But your concern touches me."

His voice belied the sentiment, and Amber swung away from him, pretending to study the water. The light was fading now and she realised that the several twin glowing objects on the water's surface belonged to caimans, their scaly bodies submerged and only their eyes showing.

Marco said quietly, "This is when the animals come to drink. If we are patient we will see others. But you will need this." He produced a small can of insect repellent, took her hand and sprayed the cool liquid down both sides of her arm, doing the same for the other, then sprayed some into his hand and smoothed it over her face and neck before doing the same for himself.

Amber sat entranced beside Marco on a convenient flat rock while birds of so many species that she finally stopped counting flew overhead, roosted in the trees or cautiously dipped their beaks into the lake's edge.

Marco knew all of their names in English as well as Spanish—yellow-knobbed curassow, sun-bittern, white-throated spadebill, fuscous flycatcher, pale-eyed pygmy-tyrant and dozens more. Some were beautiful, some strange, many sporting unbelievably bright colours. Red, green, blue, yellow and everything between.

Pink flamingos stalked en masse on the other side of the lagoon. A fox and an ant-eater slunk down to slake their thirst. A family of skittish white-tailed deer approached and warily drank, shying away from the lurking caimans with their sharp teeth.

It was dark by the time Amber and Marco returned to

the hacienda under a wide sky lit by an aloof white moon and millions of stars.

As José led the horses away Amber turned to Marco. "Thank you," she said. "It was amazing."

In the dim light she couldn't see his expression when he said, "You can thank me properly later. But first we will shower and eat. You must be hungry."

"Starving!" she admitted.

Marco laughed and put a strong, warm arm loosely about her as they walked to the house.

After showering, she put on a flared skirt and sleeveless silk blouse decorated with tiny tucks and narrow lace, then pinned up her hair and used eye shadow and lipstick, knowing the other women in the household would as usual be faultlessly groomed.

In the mirror of her dressing table she saw Marco emerge from the bathroom wearing only a towel.

When he dropped it to dress she hastily averted her eyes, but the imprint of that brief sight lingered.

Remembering the anaconda with its fearsome, sensuous beauty, both fascinating and dangerous, and the way he'd effortlessly held it helpless until it pleased him to release it, she shivered. Obviously he had learned young to dominate the animals that inhabited his domain, but had he in some mystic way absorbed some of their nature?

She wondered if she would have been able to bring herself to agree to Marco's infamous proposition if he'd been old, fat and ugly, with bad teeth. Or if she hadn't felt the inexorable pull of his undoubted attraction for women, despite trying to fight it. Her acquiescence to his ultimatum hadn't been quite so selfless as she'd liked to think.

CHAPTER NINE

MEALS at the hacienda were apparently leisurely, an opportunity to talk with other members of the family, and in the evening to exchange news of their day. It was late by her standards when Marco took her up to her room, and this time he said good night to the others, came in with her and closed the door.

"Have you recovered from your jet lag?" he asked her in a neutral voice.

She could say no, or that she was tired, but it would only delay the inevitable. "Yes," she said, annoyed that her cheeks were flushing and her voice sounded husky. "I think so."

He nodded, and considered her. "You look very lovely tonight," he said. "I like this." He touched one of the tiny pearl buttons that fastened her blouse. "It's pretty."

"It's cool," she said.

"Cool *and* pretty." His eyes laughed at her. He raised his hand and cupped her cheek, his thumb caressing her lips. "You enjoyed our afternoon?"

Amber swallowed. "You know I did. Your visitors must be blown away by their experience here. I was."

"Then perhaps—" with both hands he tipped her face to him "—you can thank me now more warmly."

Reluctant to give in easily to what appeared to be a demand for her compliance, Amber hesitated. A thought wormed into her mind. Had some of the attractive young women who toured the *hato* under his guidance taken up similar invitations from their handsome host? He'd probably been spoiled for choice.

"Is this how you expect your female visitors to express their appreciation?" she asked.

His mouth tightened, and a dangerous glint appeared in his eyes. "No," he said shortly. "Only my wife."

Then his dark head came down and his mouth exacted a sweet, subtle punishment, taking what he wanted from her, apparently uncaring that she refused to kiss him back.

When he raised his head, she stared defiantly into his glittering eyes, even when his hands slid from her cheeks to her neck and settled on her bare shoulders. "Do not test my patience too far," he warned.

"Are you threatening me?"

His hands left her. "I am trying to make this easy for you. In the pool yesterday you were not averse to my lovemaking. Why do you deliberately jab these little barbs at me?"

"Maybe it's in my nature," she retorted. "You don't really know me at all—any more than I know you." Something hard and cold coming from deep within her spurred her on. "How many women have you been with?"

"That need not concern you," he answered, his head lifting at an arrogant angle as if she'd insulted him. "I was faithful to my wife—my first wife—as I will be to you."

Of course it was none of her business. She didn't know why she'd asked, except that for some reason the possibility of being one of many made her angry.

Being reminded that Marco had been married before, to

a woman he had presumably loved and cherished, didn't help her perverse mood. "Thank you," she said.

Not that there was much she could do about it if he strayed. She was locked into this marriage, had agreed to carry out its terms and wasn't in the habit of breaking her word.

Marco didn't look at all mollified. If anything his expression had grown more austere, and she realised that her reluctant acknowledgement of his promise might have sounded like sarcasm. "I can see," he said, "that you are in no frame of mind to consummate our union tonight. I will sleep elsewhere."

Torn between a miserable awareness that she'd spoiled the delicate rapport they'd built earlier, and a savage satisfaction at routing him, Amber watched him wrench open the door and leave, snapping it shut behind him.

The satisfaction quickly drained. It had been a petty victory at best, and she suspected Marco had come out of it with more battle honours than she.

Not to mention that he would ultimately win despite her desperate efforts to salvage her pride and some measure of autonomy from this debacle. No matter how much she twisted and turned and snapped at him, or how deeply she despised herself for her body's astonishing response to his male charisma, she had no choice in the end but to surrender.

CHAPTER TEN

MARCO was gone before Amber went down for breakfast. If he'd returned to their room earlier to gather some clothes she hadn't heard him.

Señora Salzano returned her *"Buenos días"* with a restrained smile and a gracious nod. Elena returned the greeting politely but without enthusiasm, and Ana Maria jumped up to escort Amber to the table and urged her to fill her plate.

Sitting down again, Ana Maria said, "You look a little tired, Amber." Then, her eyes sparkling with mischief, she asked, "Is my brother's machismo too much for his bride?"

Amber flushed, but was saved from answering by Señora Salzano speaking sharply to her daughter in Spanish. The woman understood English better than she spoke it.

Ana Maria looked abashed and told Amber, "I didn't mean to embarrass you."

Mustering a smile, Amber shook her head. "I'm used to being teased by my sister."

Ana Maria smiled. "And *we* are sisters now, you and I— since you married my brother."

Amber spent the morning with Marco's sister on the courtyard terrace. While Ana Maria was busy with textbooks and a laptop computer, Amber read a book she'd bought at one of the stopovers on the long flight. She'd phoned her parents and assured them she was well and comfortable, and talked about the amazing wildlife with real enthusiasm.

Near lunchtime she heard the sound of a car drawing up outside, and shortly a young man appeared at the open end of the courtyard. He strode quickly across the flagstones and leapt lightly up the steps to the terrace.

Ana Maria jumped up, laughing, and ran towards him.

A wide grin on his face, he opened his arms to her and she flung herself into them, squealing, "Diego!" hugging him back and speaking in excited Spanish.

Amber uncertainly stood too. Ana Maria took the young man's hand and dragged him over to introduce them. "Diego is back early from visiting his family," she said, and then turned to him. "We were expecting you tomorrow when the next tourists are due."

"I was anxious to meet Marco's new bride," he said. "Elena told me the news." Bowing over Amber's hand, he lightly kissed it. "I see he has chosen well. She is *una belleza.*" His eyes sparkled with appreciation as well as curiosity. "I congratulate him."

Amber gave a small tug at the hand he still held, and he relinquished it with a little moue of regret.

He was probably in his late twenties and hadn't missed out on the family good looks, with thick dark hair and brown eyes, and a lady-killer smile. "So," he said. "What do you think of our little hacienda?"

Amber laughed. *Little?* "I think it's very impressive, and the birdlife and animals are simply fabulous."

He chatted for a while and left to greet his aunt.

At lunch Marco was absent. No one remarked on it, and Amber didn't want to admit her ignorance of her husband's routine or whereabouts. She gathered it was normal for the *llaneros* to start work at dawn in order to avoid the heat later in the day. If they were working far from the hacienda they would take food with them.

Diego flirted outrageously with her, making Ana Maria laugh. His aunt murmured reprovingly once or twice, but his exaggerated contrition made even her lips twitch, and he lightened Amber's mood.

Marco arrived late for dinner, stopped briefly in the dining room to apologise to his mother and greet Diego and, scarcely looking at Amber, left to get out of his dusty work clothes and have a shower.

When he reappeared, newly shaved and with his damp hair slicked back, he kissed Amber's cheek before seating himself at the head of the table. He accepted Diego's congratulations on his marriage with a nod, and after a glance at Amber cut off the younger man's fulsome compliments on his choice with a curt, "Don't embarrass my wife, Diego." Followed by something in Spanish before turning his attention to his plate.

Diego murmured, *"Perdón, por favor,* Amber,*"* seeming only slightly abashed, his eyes dancing, and she had to smile back. His light chatter made up for his cousin's taciturnity, and she was glad of the distraction.

She went upstairs early, but after donning a light lawn shift-style nightgown over matching bikini panties and removing the bedcover, she sat against the pillows leafing though fashion magazines Ana Maria had loaned her, some of them in English. She was too keyed up to concentrate on a book.

Outside she could hear men's voices, a group of *llaneros* chatting and laughing, and then music—haunting guitar music accompanying a Spanish song that seemed redolent of love and loss. Long after the music had ceased, and she'd heard Señora Salzano and Ana Maria enter their rooms, Marco hadn't appeared. She wondered if he was talking to his newly arrived cousin—or had he returned to wherever he'd slept last night?

Eventually she switched off the bedside light and tried to will herself to sleep. The room was suffused with cool moonlight, and after a while she opened her eyes and stared at the high, white ceiling with its solid supporting beams. A wave of homesickness washed over her.

Turning onto her side, she curled her legs up, and for a short while let tears flow. Then she heard the quiet turning of the doorknob, and held her breath as Marco slipped into the room and the door clicked shut behind him.

Amber closed her eyes. She had been ready to talk things out, try to come to some understanding, and was unreasonably aggrieved that he'd taken so long to follow her, as if he should have known she was waiting for him.

He made hardly a sound, but she sensed that he'd moved nearer. After minutes seemed to have passed she risked opening her eyes the tiniest slit, and saw he was standing at the window, one hand resting on the wall beside it as he leaned slightly forward, the moonlight silhouetting his proud, resolute profile and laying a silver patina on his black hair.

As if he felt her gaze he straightened and dropped his hand to his side, turning towards the bed.

Amber hastily closed her eyes again, willing her breathing to evenness.

Again there was a pause, but now he was so near she could smell the soap and aftershave he'd used, hear his breathing. Invisibly she stiffened, every nerve on the alert. Then she felt the lightest brush of something warm across her damp cheek—Marco's lips—and heard the harsh drawing in of his breath, followed by a whispered exclamation, and through her eyelids caught the sudden flaring of the bedside light as he switched it on.

She had to open her eyes then, covering them with the back of her hand and rolling over so her back was to him when he loomed over her.

He pulled her hand away and looked down at her, his lips tight. "Am I so fearsome," he said, "you must cry yourself to sleep?"

"I'm not afraid of you!" Amber injected scorn into her voice and sat up so that she was more nearly level with him. Bad enough being caught for a second time crying like a baby, let alone having him think he could intimidate her.

"You relieve my mind," he said gravely. "Then why have you been weeping into your pillow? Perhaps you missed my presence in your bed?" He shifted to sit on the side of it, facing her with his arm across her legs, his hand on the sheet beside her hip.

Amber glared. He was uncomfortably close to the mark. "What I miss is my home, my family."

"Ah." He actually looked sympathetic. "That is understandable. You have spoken to them?"

"Yes."

"Good. If you wish, you may do so every day and talk for as long as you like."

As if she needed his permission. But to be fair, he was paying the phone bill. She made a conscious effort to excuse his habitual air of command as a result of being in charge of this vast enterprise. "I'm sorry if I was a bit sharp last night," she said. "Only I felt you were pushing me into a corner, making me kiss you."

He looked at her steadily for a long moment before he

said, "Then I too am sorry, Amber." He picked up her hand that was clutching the edge of the sheet and kissed it, retaining his hold as he lowered it. His voice deepening, he said, "If you had just said no I would have respected that. I want very much to make love to you, when you are ready." He raised his other hand and brushed at her cheek with his thumb, wiping away the last trace of tears. "Have I not told you I am not a brute, to take a woman by force?"

He could have, she knew. The walls in this place were thick, the doors solid wood, and even if someone had heard her scream, no one in this house would willingly cross Marco or interfere in his marriage.

She supposed his ancestors had not been so enlightened, their women given little choice, any resistance easily and ruthlessly overcome.

The blood of the conquistadors still ran in Marco's veins. His methods might be more subtle, but when it came down to it she had no option but to meet his demands, however he couched them.

In that respect she was no different from the helpless Indian maidens who became spoils of war, or the aristocratic, sheltered *señoritas* whose marriages were arranged for dynastic reasons.

Procrastination was pointless. She took a deep breath and said, "All right. Tonight, then. Now."

Before she lost her nerve.

Marco had been looking down at the hand he held, his thumb roving back and forth over her skin. He looked up, his eyes searching as she met them with what she hoped was a fearless stare, ignoring the colony of butterflies that had taken residence in her stomach. "Why now?" he demanded, his eyes narrowing.

Amber shrugged. "It's as good a time as any. The sooner

we…start, the sooner I can get pregnant and you'll have what you wanted. And then…you said you'd let me go."

Her insides went hollow at the very thought of leaving after having his baby, but she thrust that aside to be dealt with later. Right now all she wanted was to get this over with. She didn't have to *enjoy* it.

"Well?" she challenged him belligerently.

Marco for once was apparently at a loss. At last he said, "If that is what you want."

"I said so, didn't I?" Her voice had ratcheted up a notch. Trying to loosen the knot of nervous tension that threatened to choke her, she said, "Unless you're exhausted after chasing cattle or whatever you were doing all day?"

A gleam entered his eyes. "I am not so exhausted as that."

Abruptly he stood up and began unbuttoning his white shirt, his eyes holding hers.

When he let the shirt drop to the floor her heart seemed to leap into her throat. She would have liked to ask him to turn off the light but didn't want him to know she was having an attack of shyness. As his hands went to the tooled leather belt he wore, her gaze involuntarily followed. He tugged at the silver buckle, and the belt joined his shirt on the floor. His bronzed feet were bare.

He opened the waistband of his trousers but didn't unzip them, saying, "Move over, *querida*," as he threw back the sheet.

Amber obeyed, inwardly quivering with nerves, automatically pulling down the hem of the short gown when it rode up on her thighs, then thinking how stupidly prudish that was.

The bulk of Marco's magnificent, half-naked body obscured the bedside lamp and threw the farther half of the bed into shadow. He adjusted the pillows before leaning on one elbow and surveying her like a connoisseur appraising a work of art. One he wasn't sure was worth its price.

His free hand fingered a lock of her hair and tucked it behind her ear. "You are naturally blond?" he asked.

"More so when I was a kid," she answered huskily. "I use lemon rinse when I wash it."

A smile touched his mouth. "Ah, sweet yet sharp." He leaned forward and inhaled the scent of her hair, then dropped a kiss on the top of her head, another on her forehead. With kisses he closed her eyes. His mouth wandered across her cheek to her ear, and his tongue found the small indentation below.

Amber lay perfectly still, fighting her body's responses and the sensation that she was melting inside.

Marco's hand trailed from just under her chin down her throat, paused on the pulse beating at its base, pressing gently with a finger, then moved under the satin of the nightshirt to cup her shoulder while his tongue explored the hollow his finger had discovered.

Amber forced her eyes wide open, trying to dispel the feelings he was arousing, determined not to give in to them. Somehow it was important to her self-respect that she retain control over her body even as she allowed Marco to do whatever he willed with it. He'd had his way in everything else. The only thing she could deny him was her active participation.

He lifted his head and looked at her flushed face, her stubbornly closed mouth, and she stared back at him defiantly.

"I see," he said softly. "You wish to make this a war of wills, *mi esposa*."

My wife, he was reminding her. Amber clenched her fists, held rigidly at her sides. "I'm not fighting you."

A smile holding both arrogance and irony briefly

touched his mouth. "We will see how long your *resistencia pasivo* will last."

He began unfastening her nightgown with agonising slowness. At last he parted it, revealing her breasts, that to her utter chagrin she knew were visibly reacting to his intent gaze. Lower down the minuscule panties did very little for modesty.

She heard Marco expel a breath, and turned her head aside. *"¡Exquisita!"* he said. "You are even more beautiful than I had dreamed."

He circled each peaking breast with a finger, then began drawing closer to the centre of the right one, which throbbed, aching for his touch.

When it came, she dug her teeth into her lower lip, clasping at the sheet with her hands as he teased and tormented. Then his hair brushed like silk against her skin and she felt his mouth, his tongue, caressing, tasting, stroking. Involuntarily her eyes closed tight and she forced herself to stay still until she could bear it no longer without betraying herself, and cried out, "Stop!"

He did, to take her chin in his hand and look into her eyes, his own glittering with night fire, his cheeks darkened, a faint sheen on his forehead.

She knew he saw the flush that warmed her face, the glazed look in her eyes. His gaze shifted to her mouth, swollen where she'd bitten into it, and then his head came down, his lips gently taking her bruised one between them, his tongue moistening the small hurt, easing it.

She felt his bare chest against the pebble-hard evidence of her unwilling arousal and was torn between shame and her growing desire to reciprocate the tender, tantalising kisses he was bestowing on her mouth.

He began kissing her throat, her shoulders, the inner

crook of her left elbow, the smooth skin over the tiny veins in her wrist. He kissed each finger in turn, then took one in his mouth and sucked on it, his tongue playing around it, and gave it a painless nip with his teeth before returning his attention to her breasts.

She heard her own breath quicken, and could do nothing to hide it or the hammering of her heart when Marco put his palm over it, while his mouth wreaked havoc on her senses, until she gave a small, involuntary moan and moved restlessly on the bed.

Marco gave a brief, breathy laugh, and his mouth moved lower while she clenched her teeth. She hadn't known that her navel was an erogenous zone, but then, every inch of her skin seemed to be equally so. Everywhere he touched with his mouth, his hands, his body, her nerves seethed with answering desire. When his hand glided over the satin panties and cupped her between her legs, she knew he'd recognise the proof that she was indeed ready for him. But he didn't simply tear off the last barrier between them, instead dispensing with his own trousers first, then slipping a finger inside her panties and beginning a slow, relentless stroking.

"Don't," she whispered, despite the reluctant pleasure he was giving her, draining her will. Her head thrashed from side to side in desperate negation, even as her legs parted of their own accord. *"Please!"*

Immediately he stopped what he'd been doing, his hand moving to her breast, caressing, gently tweaking, and that was almost worse—her body was bathed in fire, every skin cell alive, needy, longing, while her mind frantically fought for control. Her lips parted on a long drawn-in breath, and then Marco's mouth was on hers, open and hot in a merciless, passionate, searing kiss, his tongue an instrument of erotic torture, sending her mindless, while she could feel between her thighs the hard, proud crux of his manhood demanding entry.

When his mouth left hers Amber was dizzy, floating on a sea of wanting, needing. The tumbled sheets, the bed, the world itself seemed far away. She hardly felt Marco remove her panties, and when he poised himself over her, his eyes like black jewels, his male scent an aphrodisiac, his mouth rigid with superhuman control, she stared back at him with fierce, silent craving.

He entered her slowly, as if afraid of hurting her, and she couldn't help lifting to him a little, wanting him deeper, wanting him to fill her, wanting him…

She heard the harsh sigh of satisfaction he breathed against her cheek, and then he thrust powerfully, deeply, lifting his head to watch her face, and she closed her eyes, closed herself around him, felt her body convulse, lost herself in unbelievable, shuddering delight, heard her own voice cry out wordlessly and at last raised her arms and wrapped them tight about his shoulders.

CHAPTER ELEVEN

DIMLY she was aware that Marco was speaking in Spanish, his voice low, sexy, urgent. She heard him say her name— Amber—and then *querida, bella, muy buena,* and other words that she didn't recognise.

Then he gave a long, guttural moan and she felt his muscles tense under her hands, his body quiver as it was taken over in his turn by the uncontrollable pleasure that was like no other. Amber clung to him, her fingers unconsciously digging into his flesh, her own pleasure was heightened by the knowledge that Marco shared it, that he was buried deep inside her, their limbs twined about each other, their bodies fused together as if nothing would ever part them.

She was still having tiny aftershocks when Marco finally collapsed against her, then rolled over, holding her to him, the movement intensifying the sensation so that she let slip a small, surprised, "Oh!"

He must have felt the rhythmic spasms she couldn't stop, and his hands shifted from her waist to stroke over the curves below and hold her at the top of her thighs while he rocked her, encouraging her, and she felt him harden again inside her. Half-horrified and yet impelled by primeval instinct that held her in thrall, she moved against him, driving herself to the goal she knew was within reach, felt him match her rhythm, find the apex, until they fell together into the void once more and she couldn't stop her whimpering cries.

Exhausted, she dropped her head against Marco's dampened shoulder, inhaling a salty aroma mixed with the essence of his skin scent.

Marco stroked her tumbled hair, murmuring, *"¡Maravillosa!"* Marvellous.

He kissed her cheek, then pressed a long, slow kiss on her mouth before easing himself away.

Her body felt weightless, as if it were no longer flesh and blood but something ethereal, drifting on air.

He tended her, found her panties and her nightdress and covered the nakedness he'd so thoroughly explored. "Go to sleep," he whispered, and kissed her drooping eyelids closed. Then he kissed her again on her mouth, his lips lingering, tender. Moments later his arm came around her and his hard, lean body warmed hers.

She gave a long, luxurious sigh and slid into sleep.

Sunlight and the twittering of birds woke her. The pillow next to hers was dented, the sheet cold. She realised she'd missed hearing Marco get up and leave, even missed breakfast. Hastily she scrambled from the bed and made for the bathroom and a lukewarm shower.

Coming out, she grabbed a towel and caught her reflection in the mirror—saw that her lips were full and red, her eyes luminous and languorous. Bedroom eyes.

At the washbasin she rinsed her face over and over with cold water, hoping to eliminate the telltale signs.

Downstairs she apologised to Señora Salzano, who

insisted on asking Filipa to bring a tray for her, saying, "You must eat, to give Marco a strong healthy *niño*."

"I'm not pregnant, señora!"

"Who knows? A *bebé* does not make its presence known *inmediatamente*."

Amber realised the *señora* might be right. The thought gave her peculiar feelings—a flash of panic, followed by something much more complex, compounded of wonder and denial and a flutter of excitement.

Ana Maria was studying, apparently, and there was no sign of Diego or Elena. After eating her delayed breakfast, Amber took the tray to the kitchen herself, then went upstairs to transfer more film to her computer, and spent the morning editing yesterday's pictures. The editing programme was new to her, and she was still working it out by trial and error when Marco arrived for lunch, startling her and making her realise how quickly the time had passed.

He strode across the room to stand behind her chair. His hand caressed her shoulder and he bent to place a kiss on her cheek. He smelled of leather and dust and the hot sun. "What are you doing?" he asked.

She told him, and he said, "Something to send your family?"

"Not only them. I thought while I was here I'd try my hand at making a documentary for television. I might be able to sell it back in New Zealand if it's good enough."

Marco's hand dropped. "Lunch is on the table," he said, and headed for the bathroom.

Apparently Diego had been with Marco, checking a camp where the next group of tourists had booked two nights. They talked about it at the table.

"They sleep in tents?" Amber queried.

Diego flashed her his supersmile. "There is a lodge to

keep our visitors safe. Is bad for business if the customers get eaten." He made his hands into claws and pantomimed a snarling wild beast, then sat back, grinning as Amber and Ana Maria burst out laughing.

Amber caught Marco watching her, unsmiling, a strange expression in his eyes.

Diego said, "We take guns along as a precaution, but if the tourists do as we say there is no problem. Personally," he added darkly, his expression changing, "I would rather shoot one of them than a puma or jaguar, if they get in its way."

"Unfortunately—" Marco's dry voice broke in as Amber raised her brows in disbelief "—shooting our guests is also not good for business, Diego."

Diego shrugged. "I tell them there are plenty of *hombres estúpidos* in the world but not so many pumas left, so I must take care of the pumas first. They laugh, but maybe there is a bit of doubt." He held up a thumb and forefinger no more than a centimetre apart. "*Diminuto*. Is enough." He grinned again at Amber.

She said, "I'm sure the customers love you, Diego." He must be a hit with the women.

"Anytime you want your own guided tour, *bella señora*," he said, "I am happy to show you."

"I'd love to film a puma in the wild," Amber told him. "Or a jaguar." Impulsively she asked, "Is there any chance I could join your group tomorrow?"

"*Sí!*" Diego's eyes lit up, but Marco cut him off with an unequivocal, "No!"

Disappointed, and irked at the imperious veto, Amber demanded, "Why not?"

Something flashed in Marco's eyes, but he said calmly, "Be patient, *querida*. I will take you myself to the *campamento*, when it is empty of strangers and we will be alone." He smiled slightly, in his eyes a deep, challenging spark, and it was as though only the two of them were in the room. A tiny shiver spiralled through her, and she couldn't speak.

Could the others at the table read the silent reminder of last night? She saw Elena glance from her to Marco, then dip her head and dig her fork into a piece of beef.

Ana Maria said, "You have had no *luna de miel,* have you, Amber? Though the *campamento* is not…um…*muy lujoso…*" She asked Marco, "What is the word?"

Amber too turned to her husband inquiringly. Neither phrase had yet entered her limited Spanish vocabulary.

"It is not luxurious," he supplied, and to Amber, "My sister does not think it suitable for a honeymoon."

A honeymoon? Amber stared at him. He lifted a dark brow, saying, "We can talk about it later." Then he turned to Elena and they began discussing the preparations for the visitors.

Amber drew in a breath. If this had been a normal marriage she'd have jumped at the offer of a honeymoon in the jungle among free-roaming animals. When she and her sister were younger they'd sometimes camped with their parents during school holidays, at a beach or national park.

She was suddenly overwhelmed by a longing for lush green paddocks where sleek, fat cattle and woolly white sheep grazed; for cool, thick, green bush that held no dangers, and deserted beaches where it was safe to walk barefoot on miles of smooth, soft sand.

Ana Maria murmured to her, "Amber, are you all right?"

Despite the girl's lowered voice Marco must have heard. His head turned sharply from Elena towards Amber in midsentence, and when she instinctively looked at him his gaze was piercing.

She returned her attention to his sister and forced a smile to her lips. "I'm fine," she said.

"You look a little tired," Ana Maria told her.

"There is a reason for that," Marco said.

Ana Maria's face brightened with delighted comprehension, and Diego gave a knowing chuckle.

Marco went on, "My wife is unused to our climate and she has been tiring herself with her explorations. Today, *querida,* you must have a nice long siesta."

Tempted to tell him she would do exactly as she pleased, perhaps go for a nice long walk or take Domitila for a nice long gallop across the *llano,* Amber kept the smile in place, the devoted bride in front of his family.

After Filipa had cleared the plates from the table, Marco was the first to rise, coming round to pull out Amber's chair and take her hand so that she had no choice but to accompany him upstairs. Behind them she heard Diego murmur something, followed by a giggle from Ana Maria and then Elena's voice, short and sharp in rapid Spanish.

When Marco had closed the door of their room behind them, Amber tugged her hand from his and crossed to the window, staring at the expanse of blue-green grassland drying to pale brown in the sun, with the inevitable flock of birds wheeling under a cloudless sky, then dropping as one into a distant clump of twisted trees.

"Come," Marco said from somewhere behind her. "Ana Maria is right. You should rest."

"I'm not tired." Her voice was brittle, and she didn't turn from her stance at the window. After all, she had slept late that morning.

"No?" Silently Marco had crossed the huge rug that covered the old boards, and his hands descended lightly on her shoulders. "*Bueno.* I too do not wish to sleep."

She felt his fingers push aside her hair, which she'd left loose before hurrying downstairs, and then his lips were on her neck, pressing little kisses in one spot, then another, and another. His hand slipped the wide boat-neck of her cotton top off her shoulder and he kissed the smooth curve, his hair cool and soft against her cheek. His other hand went to her midriff, sliding under the shirt.

Amber closed her eyes. Already he was aroused, and unwilling or not, so was she. Memories of last night danced in tantalising, erotic pictures behind her eyelids, and her body remembered too wanton and wayward, ignoring her mind's effort to assert control.

What was the use? Marco already knew he could break down her inadequate defences, bring her to humiliating, quivering acquiescence—and more than that, much more: to a primeval, raging lust for a man she surely should loathe.

His ancestors had conquered with fire and sword, cruel and rapacious, taking what they fancied—gold, jewels, land…and women. Marco's weapons were his hands, his mouth, his naked body, his intimate knowledge of female anatomy—in short, his skill at pleasing a woman—to achieve his conquest over her. She should be grateful that it was a gentle though ruthless seduction rather than a brutal, uncaring slaking of crude sexual appetite.

Even now, as he turned her in his arms and she opened her eyes, saw the fierce masculine beauty of his face, the glitter of passion in his eyes, she knew her own face reflected the fever of desire, her skin going taut and hot, her eyelids involuntarily falling again as he bent to her, his mouth working dark magic, spinning her into an abyss of mounting, dangerous sexual hunger.

He swept her up in his arms, and she wound her own arms

about his neck, her head nestled against his shoulder until he reached the bed and tumbled onto it, still holding her.

With a kind of bitter resignation, she thought hazily that if she couldn't rouse enough self-respect to resist, she might as well enjoy the moment. When he set about swiftly removing her clothes, she tore at the buttons on his shirt, and it was her hands that fumbled with the buckle of his belt, unzipped his trousers, helped haul them off. She wanted him, wanted to be held close, kissed, stroked, wanted to explore his body with her hands and mouth as he had hers last night. Wanted the sweet oblivion that only he could give her, when for a little time nothing mattered but this need to have each other, hold each other, giving and receiving the greatest physical pleasure a man and woman could experience.

When it came, her whole body stiffened in Marco's embrace, and her parted mouth drew in a breath and held it until her body released its tension and wave after wave engulfed her in delight, gifting her the fulfilment she craved. She felt his answering surge inside her, and thought she would die, drowned in exquisite sensation. Surely no one could bear this much pure enjoyment, going on and on for so long?

Then it was over, and she lay panting, dizzy, spent, unable to move, her hair tumbled around and over her face, her limbs boneless, while reality slowly trickled back into her consciousness.

Marco leaned over her, his hair rumpled. She vaguely remembered burying her fingers in the thickness of it, holding him to her as his tongue did exciting things to her breasts. He looked pleased, triumphant. His hand lifted her hair away from her face and he smiled down at her—a lazy, satisfied smile—then kissed her softly, erotically, savouring her mouth with all the finesse of a connoisseur tasting some exotic new dish.

Then he gathered her into his arms and tucked her head against his shoulder, stroking her hair. It felt good, her resting place against his skin warm and comfortable. She was utterly filled with a sense of wellbeing, of contentment. For now, she refused to think about what had brought her here, or what was to come. On that defiant thought she dozed off.

Marco's movement woke her sometime later as he carefully eased himself away and left the bed, to pull on his trousers with his back to her.

Opening her eyes, she drew in a quick, horrified breath as she saw the red marks on his shoulders. She sat up, dragging the sheet over her bare breasts.

Instantly he turned. "I'm sorry I woke you. I have work to do." Taking in her expression, he said, "What is the matter?"

"I...your shoulders," she said. "Did I...?" She looked down at her fingernails, which perfectly matched the crescent-shaped red indentations she'd seen on his skin.

Her hands went over her mouth in embarrassment, then she quickly lowered them to readjust the sheet.

Marco laughed. "Yes, you have put your mark on me, *mi tigresa pequeña. De nada,*" he said, picking up his shirt to pull it on over the small wounds. "Do not worry. They are proof of your affection for your husband, no?"

His *little tigress* sent him a hostile glance. It had no visible effect. He laughed again, and with the shirt still open he bent over to kiss the top of her head. Drawing away, he pulled her inadequate covering down a little and said huskily, "You have the marks of *amor* on you too." She followed his gaze and saw two patches of pinkened flesh on the upper slopes of her breasts.

Marco perched on the edge of the bed and leaned towards her, planting a kiss on each telltale sign, making her catch her breath against the dissolution of her insides. "Such delicate skin," he murmured. "I will try to take more care next time."

Abruptly he stood up. "You tempt me to neglect my duties. But unfortunately I must leave you, *mi amante*."

When he'd gone Amber found her Spanish dictionary and looked up *amante*.

It meant *lover*.

Or possibly *mistress*.

It was no use trying to pretend she was indifferent to Marco's lovemaking, though she told herself she was merely fulfilling her part of the bargain they had made.

The day she informed him as neutrally as she could that she wasn't pregnant, he merely nodded and said, "There is plenty of time, *querida*."

One afternoon she summoned the willpower to turn him down when he made a move during siesta, saying she wasn't in the mood, it was too hot. Marco shrugged, said calmly, "As you wish, of course," and moved to the other side of the bed, to lie on his back with his hands behind his head, staring at the ceiling, the fan in the centre sending cooling air over the bed.

Amber turned her head away and tried to persuade herself the jittery tension and restlessness she felt had nothing to do with sexual frustration.

After a while Marco got up and said, "I'm going to swim." He didn't invite her along, and she wouldn't let herself ask. She swam with Ana Maria quite often, and sometimes Diego joined them, splashing them and horsing about until they ganged up on him and fought back. Even

Elena joined them now and then. But Marco often seemed to prefer having the pool to himself.

The next day he didn't appear for lunch or siesta time, but when he followed her to bed that night and reached for her Amber discovered in herself something she had never suspected. In answer to Marco's gentle consideration she responded with a ferocious, frantic ardour. Driven by confused feelings of frustrated need and the hard, cold lump of frozen tears that seemed to be her heart, she kissed with furious passion, teased with her hair, her hands, her body, used his body to heighten her own desire and, like the tigress he'd called her, bit and scratched, turning their bed into a battlefield, though it only made him laugh in pleased surprise. Which finally freed her inner rage.

She was lying on top of him then, her breasts filling his hands, and she began pummelling his chest with her fists, her teeth clenched, until he caught her wrists in his big hands and turned her over, trapping her with her wrists pinned against the pillows as he thrust into her again and again with all the violence and heat and fury that she craved. The world exploded around them and she lost herself, her mind, her body shattering into a million shards of glittering, unbelievable, seemingly unending pleasure until she fell into a dark, velvety void.

A deep animal growl came from Marco's throat as he reached his own climax, culminating in a long, harsh sigh.

It was minutes before he released her, and she returned to a consciousness of where she was and what had just happened. Finally she rolled onto her stomach, appalled at her own behaviour, too mortified to face Marco, yet still tingling all over with the luxurious, lethargic aftermath of frenzied, out-of-this-world sex.

Marco touched her hair, then swept his hand slowly

down her spine, over the curve of her behind, and back up again. He went on lazily stroking her with his warm, soothing hand, murmuring to her in musical Spanish until she drifted into sleep.

Amber phoned her parents each week, confining the conversation mostly to life on the *hato* and the fun she was having filming its animal inhabitants. It wasn't difficult to wax lyrical about the wildlife and the food, the harsh beauty of the *llanos*. She also spoke to her sister, both of them skating over the reason she was so far from home. Amber was unsure if Rickie was around to hear.

Azure put Benny on the line, and Amber realised how much she missed the little boy. Listening to his baby babbling, she thought if she felt this strongly about her nephew, how could she ever leave her own baby?

Would Marco cast her off as soon as she'd fulfilled her promise to give him a child? He'd said she could leave then, but also that in his faith marriage was forever, and surely sexually at least he was satisfied? If they had a baby together that must create a stronger bond.

Tourist parties and backpackers came and went, sometimes with a few days between.

A bird-watching club from Britain stayed for several days, excited by the variety of species they spotted in so short a time. Then a trio of scientists studying the climatology and ecology of the *llanos* dined with the family and talked with Marco and Diego about balancing cattle management and wildlife preservation.

Amber realised that Señora Salzano quietly kept her hands on the reins of the household, ensuring the hacienda was clean and well kept despite its age, the guest accommodation serviced by women who lived in neat, pink-washed houses nearby. She oversaw supplies and meals and worked with Elena to ensure their guests' comfort. And, she ran a project to make white cheese commercially along with some of the *llanero* wives.

Every member of the family had their responsibilities. Amber sometimes felt superfluous to requirements, but offered help where she could.

Something inside her seemed to have broken on that night of ferocious lovemaking with Marco. She hoped it wasn't her spirit. Their sexual encounters were intense; her rage had faded and the ice around her heart was melting.

Marco was unfailingly thoughtful and courteous, although sometimes she sensed a restraint in him, as if he were holding back. Occasionally she caught him looking at her with a brooding expression, his eyes black and un-readable, his mouth taut, perhaps impatient for news of a pregnancy.

If only she could forgive him for the way he'd manipulated her, trapped her, might they build a true relationship based on sexual compatibility and parenting a child—or children?

Any child of this mockery of a marriage deserved a stable, happy home—not two parents at loggerheads. She could keep on sniping at Marco, hold on to her bitter re-sentment and turn into a shrew, continually carping on how unwillingly he'd got her where he wanted her. She might manage to hurt him a little, but in the end she'd hurt herself more, become the kind of person she would never want to be, unhappy and full of spite.

Or she could accept there was no way out of this situa-tion and try to turn it into something more than a conve-nient arrangement.

One Sunday the family piled into two cars and drove to

a white adobe church where a priest came once a month to say Mass for the *rancheros* on their parcels of land.

Marco introduced Amber to the silver-haired priest before the service. Afterwards a dozen or so men came to shake Marco's hand and be introduced to his bride. Women hung back with shy smiles, children either clinging to their skirts or scampering around after each other.

The priest took Marco aside, and whatever Marco said made the other man frown and shake his head, glancing at Amber, who stood waiting beside Señora Salzano. But then he gave an apparently reluctant nod and raised his hand in a blessing before Marco rejoined the family.

Amber waited until they were alone to ask, "Does the priest disapprove of me?"

"No. The padre is displeased that I have not yet arranged a church wedding."

"A *church* wedding?"

"Here in Venezuela couples must have a civil ceremony for legal reasons, but it is traditional to be married in a church afterwards. That is regarded as the real wedding."

"He doesn't feel we're really married?" After a little thought, Amber said slowly, "What about your mother?"

"She is religious. For her it is important."

Maybe that was the reason the *señora* seemed rather distant with Amber, though always gracious. And why Concepcion, though respectful, often looked at her with polite disdain, and at Marco with sad disapproval.

Did Marco regard their marriage as real? she wondered. Maybe he'd left himself a loophole. He might still be able to marry again if he sent her home.

She began to adjust to life on the *hato,* enlivened by Ana

Maria and Diego, both happy to help her with her Spanish, which she studied every afternoon. Señora Salzano gradually became less aloof, seeming pleased and approving when Amber tried to converse with her in broken Spanish or asked to help with some household task. Even Elena accepted her presence on a day trip with a new bunch of tourists, pointing out good subjects for filming. Although Elena's manner remained cool, she seemed a different being, casually dressed with her hair in a ponytail, her make-up disappearing in the sun.

Again Amber had to tell Marco there was no pregnancy. And again he said there was plenty of time.

She started filming the day-to-day life of the ranch. The brown-skinned, sun-wrinkled *llaneros* saddled up at first light, Stetson-type hats on their heads but, astonishingly, many wearing a type of sandals on their feet. They rode out to move the wandering cattle to fresh pasture or bring them into the yards near the hacienda, where they would separate and brand the yearlings, draft some beasts for sale or butcher a few for the hacienda's meals.

One day she filmed them as they brought in a small herd of the feral horses that roamed the plains, and the *llaneros* set about taming their new mounts, making critical comments on one another's efforts and laughing whenever a rider hit the dusty ground.

Ana Maria took Amber to watch, saying, "In the old days they used whips and spurs, but Marco won't allow that. Some of the old *llaneros* laughed at him, said no horse would obey until it was properly broken and afraid not to. But he showed them they were wrong."

A snorting, white-eyed mare, according to Marco the matriarch of the herd, had been driven in with the others, but eluded all efforts to catch her. Marco and a couple of men had isolated her and she was alone in a large corral. A day later Marco rode into it and they closed the gate behind him. Ana Maria had persuaded Amber that his technique was worth seeing.

A coiled rope hung on his saddle. He had his horse approaching the mare at a walk. The *llaneros* perching or leaning on the surrounding rails fell silent.

The wild horse shifted as the other drew near, and when they were a few metres apart she lifted her head and galloped off to another corner of the enclosure.

Marco and his mount followed. Everywhere she went, horse and rider remained at her side, sometimes turning tightly to evade lashing hooves and threatening teeth, but always coming back to mimic her movements.

Eventually the mare seemed to tire, realising there was no escape. She stood with her head down and Marco reached over to touch her at the shoulder, talking quietly, soothingly and gently rubbing.

She twitched away, but took only a couple of steps, and when he did it again she only turned her head as if asking what he was up to.

Marco dismounted, still talking, the lasso in his hand, and although she eyed him suspiciously, when he put a hand again on the horse's strong neck she shuddered and tossed her head but didn't run.

Marco appeared to have endless patience, and Amber found she was holding her breath when he tried to slip the noose over the horse's head. The mare evaded it and trotted to another corner of the corral. He followed on foot, his own horse plodding after him. Maintaining eye contact, he went on murmuring, stroking, and after a few more feints he was able to slip the noose over the mare's head.

She tried to shake it off, then ran, but Marco vaulted

onto the other horse, following as before, gradually short-ening the restraint until, miraculously, he had the wild mare trotting alongside him, apparently happily.

In the following days Amber filmed him working the horse, persuading her to trust him, until he had her trotting in a circle. She ceased backing away at his approach, and soon was following along when he walked the other horse.

Then he tried a saddle, which she did her best to buck off, and only when she had accepted that, he mounted her for the first time.

The mare trembled at the strange sensation, turned its head and made a tight circle, apparently in an effort to see its rider, then kicked out, trying to dislodge him. Marco stayed as if glued to the saddle. Within a week he had the mare obeying his every command.

Marco's way with females, it seemed, extended even to horses.

Ana Maria suggested Amber show her edited videos to the family on the big TV screen in the *sala*. Diego and Ana Maria were predictably lavish with praise, and Marco and his mother seemed impressed.

Finally even Elena said reluctantly, "They look...quite professional!"

Amber forgave her for the obvious surprise, pleased at the young woman's reluctant respect. "It's a top-of-the-range camera," she said. "And I learned a lot about filming from the people I used to work with."

Diego said, "We could use some clips from them on our Web site—if you allow it, Amber."

"You'd be very welcome," Amber told him warmly. "Tell me which ones you want."

* * *

A few days later, after she'd been swimming with Ana Maria, Elena and Diego, as they returned to the house the two young women fell behind, gossiping about fashion.

Amber said to Diego, "Elena is getting used to me, I think. She seemed a bit…shy, at first."

"Shy?" Diego laughed and glanced back. Leaning closer, he whispered, "I think my poor cousin hoped Marco would choose her."

"Choose her?" She looked at him inquiringly.

"Marry her."

"They're cousins!" Amber stopped to face him so abruptly she stumbled and bumped against him.

Diego steadied her. "Elena is cousin to Marco's wife— I mean his first wife." Then anxiously he asked, "You know he has been married before?"

"Of course I know."

The other two caught up with them, Ana asking, "Are you all right, Amber?"

"Fine." Amber tried not to look at Elena as Diego dropped his hands. "I tripped, that's all."

The four of them entered the house together and separated to dress. When Amber reached the bedroom, Marco was standing at the window, already showered and dressed in a white shirt open at the neck, with dark trousers.

He turned, taking in the towel tucked over her swimsuit, and her bared legs. "What were you and Diego talking about?" he asked as she crossed to the wardrobe. He must have seen them in the courtyard. "Secrets?"

"No! Nothing really." Relaying Diego's revelation would be unfair to Elena.

"Don't take my cousin's compliments too seriously," Marco said. "He is *un coqueto,* likes to flirt."

"I know that." Amber found a blouse and skirt in the big

wardrobe. A little nettled, she said, "He told me Elena is a cousin by marriage."

"*Sí*. That makes her family. Her father died when she was seventeen. There was very little money left for her or her mother. Elena took a degree in business administration, and she is very useful here."

So he'd offered her a home and a job, probably paid her way through university. "What about her mother?" Amber asked. "There was nothing useful for her to do here?"

Rather coolly he said, "She did not want to move from the house she had lived in since she was a bride. She prefers to stay there with her memories."

It must have been a happy marriage. Amber wondered if Marco's parents had been happy together. A large framed photo of them on their wedding day, posed rather stiffly and smiling at the camera, hung in the *sala*.

Struck by a thought, she said, "What happened to your wedding photographs? And your son's photos? I haven't seen any pictures of them around."

"They are safe. Before I brought you here I asked my mother to remove those on display. It did not seem…tactful to leave them."

"Oh." He'd been thinking about her feelings. "But surely you miss them—I mean, their photographs. I'd understand if you want them put back."

He gave her a penetrating look. "*De nada,*" he said dismissively. "Their images live in my heart." He touched his hand to the place, and Amber could think of nothing more to say, shamed by a pang of envy in her own heart.

She turned and walked to her computer, open as she'd left it before going to the pool, the screen blank. She pressed the start button and the screen sprang to life with her latest effort at editing her videos.

Marco came to her side. "You are very good at this," he said.

"Thank you. There's so much to film here. But..." She hesitated. "I had a feeling you didn't like my plan to make a documentary and send it to New Zealand—if I can find someone to buy it."

"*Send* it? I thought you meant after—" He paused, then gave a soft little laugh. "Perhaps I misunderstood. You may film as much as you like."

Misunderstood? Light dawned. He'd thought she meant when she returned home after her role here was finished.

That night, as she lay against his chest after making love, Marco said, "We have no visitors this week. I will take you to the *campamento* as I promised."

CHAPTER TWELVE

THE *campamento* was a two-storey building with a wide balcony running along its length that gave a view of a tranquil lake. There were two big rooms with bunks, but the one Marco ushered Amber into was smaller, boasting two queen-size beds shrouded in mosquito nets, and its own bathroom.

At sunset they sat on the balcony drinking wine, and watched dozens of flamingos at the edge of the lake standing statue-like until something in the water disturbed them and they took off in a panic-stricken pink cloud.

Marco handed Amber binoculars and she saw the caiman, frustrated in its quest for prey, turn with a petulant flick of its tail and submerge, its body scarcely rippling the water. A turtle sat unperturbed on a broken, dead branch near the water, and rainbow-feathered parrots flocked, chattering, in the nearby trees.

Stunning scarlet, black or green ibis flew down to dip their long beaks in the water, and a group of monkeys approached, scattering when the three-metre-long caiman leaped at and very nearly caught one, ending up snapping in frustration on the shore.

The next day Marco collected fishing gear and took

Amber on a leisurely river trip in a flat-bottomed boat, motoring gently through blankets of mauve water hyacinths, across which jacana—brilliant yellow beneath their wings, black on top—daintily trod as though walking on the water. Kingfishers dived for their dinner, and pinkish freshwater dolphins performed elegant synchronised leaps. Otters glided by or floated on their backs, and wading birds almost five feet tall stalked along the river bank. "Jabiru," Marco called them, and pointed out a flock of whistling ducks.

Shaded by trees where yellow butterflies were as numerous as leaves, he stopped and they fished from the boat. Amber caught a saucer-size silver-and-apricot fish with a huge mouth and fearsome teeth. Torn between pride in her catch and sadness at the plight of the fish as Marco efficiently dispatched it with a quick blow to its head on the side of the boat and tossed it into a bucket, she asked, "What is it?"

"Piranha," he said nonchalantly, and she recoiled, beset by memories of lurid tales and old TV movies of hapless minor characters or evil arch-criminals being devoured in minutes by hordes of piranha.

"They are good eating," Marco said, "but bony. We need more to make a meal."

Back at the *campamento,* instead of dining in the big room lit by oil lamps, he built a fire on sand near the water and barbecued their catch, serving it up with corn patties and plantain.

In the bedroom afterwards they made love in a leisurely, languorous fashion, miles from any human eyes and ears, to the chittering, cawing and hooting of night birds and the booming calls of howler monkeys.

As she lay against him, replete, in the distance Amber

heard a deep roar, and lifted her head to listen as it was answered by another.

"Jaguars," Marco told her, stroking her hip. "The female is calling for a mate."

"This is the mating season?"

Marco gave a low laugh. "For the jaguar there is no particular season. Like us. But the male must wait until the female indicates she is receptive to his attentions. They are solitary creatures, coming together only for a short time to mate."

And stayed together just long enough to make babies, Amber thought.

The following day when they strolled along the lakeside, Marco pointed out the clear prints of a jaguar among the bird prints and snake trails.

Every day brought new discoveries and showed Amber new aspects of her husband. He could move as silently as a ghost through the tall grass of the plains or the green thickets of palms and bushes, and from twenty paces he could spot a green iguana hiding among the leaves of a tree, or an armadillo snuffling around its roots.

Although he carried a gun and a knife during their excursions, he had a passionate and protective love for his homeland, its wild creatures and its displaced indigenous population, as well as for his own heritage, and wrestled with problems of providing justice and fairness for all while preserving the economic base of the country.

She learned more about the complications of South American politics than she'd ever seen in the news. And more about her husband—his childhood on the *llanos,* his introduction in his teens to the wider world and the family's other business interests, his father's death and Marco's expansion of those interests to safeguard the family while redressing past wrongs, even against the advice and grumblings of old-guard friends and family.

One night she dared to ask, "Tell me about your wife."

She was lying in the crook of his arm while he absently stroked her hair. The stroking stopped, and after a short silence he said, "You are my wife, Amber."

"You know who I mean. I don't even know her name."

He was silent so long she thought he was going to refuse. Finally he said, "Her name was Emilia. She was very young when we married—barely nineteen. I too was young—it seems now a long time ago. She was pretty and sweet-natured, a good mother. I had known her since we were children. I think both our families expected we would marry one day, although nothing was ever said aloud."

"But you loved her?" She couldn't imagine Marco being pressured into marriage.

"Everyone loved Emilia. And she gave me Aurelio, our son, the most precious thing in the world to both of us."

He fell quiet and Amber said softly, "Aurelio. It's a nice name." Tentatively she asked, "What happened to them?"

"An accident." His voice thickened. "We were in Barinhas. I had a meeting with some politicians and landowners there, and Emilia wanted to take Aurelio shopping. He was growing at an astonishing rate, always needing new clothes or shoes."

Even now there was a note of pride in his voice. He paused again before going on. "We had arranged to meet for lunch once the meeting was over. I came out of the building where it had been held and saw them on the other side of the road. I waved. So...*stupidly!*" His voice grew harsh. "Aurelio was usually a sensible boy, but not used to the city. I remember how his face lit up, and his smile...he had such a smile, like the sun coming out on a cloudy horizon. Emilia had her arms full with parcels and bags, and anyway he thought he was too big to hold his mother's hand. I saw him step off the kerb without looking, but I had no time to shout at him, send him back, before a truck came around the corner..."

Amber held her breath, her stomach knotting, and wished she hadn't started this.

"I was too far away to do anything," Marco said, his voice now devoid of all emotion, but his accent becoming stronger. "I could see what was going to happen. Emilia—poor, brave Emilia—saw too. She dropped her parcels, her handbag, and dived—she seemed to be flying—to reach Aurelio, save him, get him out of the way. She must have known she would be killed. But it was no use. They both died instantly." His flat tone turning to harsh despair. "It all seemed so slow, and yet I could do *nothing!*"

"Oh, Marco!" Amber put her arms about him, offering what comfort she could, unable to imagine how he'd felt when his wife and child were killed before his eyes.

Tears filled her own eyes. "It wasn't your fault!"

"Everyone told me that," Marco said wearily. "It makes no difference."

Her tears spilled onto his skin, and he touched her face. "Amber...you are crying for me?"

"All of you," she said shakily, trying to wipe the tears away with one hand, trying to stop. "You and Aurelio and Emilia."

And maybe she was crying for herself too because, she realised, somewhere along the rocky road of their unconventional relationship she had fallen in love with this complicated, multifaceted man, who didn't love her and surely never would. She could give him her heart, her life. But his heart lay in a cold grave with his adored son and the gentle, courageous and selfless woman who had been destined for him from childhood—his beloved, *real* wife.

"Don't," Marco said, brushing his fingers across her wet cheeks. "They are beyond hurt, and I have become accustomed to mine. These things do not leave one, but they are past." He kissed her, holding her face in his hands. "You, Amber, have the power to give me happiness again. And I want you also to be happy." He kissed her once more. "I will do my best to make it so."

On their last day they caught a glimpse of a jaguar, its tawny coat marked with irregular circles, but it disappeared with a flick of its tail before Amber could get a shot of it with her camera.

Later they heard roaring quite close, and after hunting around for spoor Marco promised her a better opportunity.

Just before dusk the jaguars began to call again and, following the sound, Marco led Amber on a twisting route from the lake to a place where they peered through screening bushes at a magnificent spotted jaguar about twenty metres off, basking in the remains of the sunlight, flicking its tail and occasionally showing long, curved teeth to let out a full-throated roar, its ears twitching. As Amber focused her video camera an answering roar came from somewhere not far off.

"She awaits her mate," Marco whispered. "He is close now."

Within minutes a long, dark shadow rustled the grass and bushes, and a sleek black form materialised, emitting a low growl.

Marco had told her that black jaguars were sometimes born among a litter of spotted siblings, and she caught her breath at its sinuous, dangerous magnificence.

The female immediately leapt up and faced the intruder,

snarling and being snarled at in return, both animals lashing their tails and showing their curved, pointed teeth. To Amber it didn't look like a love match.

The jaguars circled warily, feinting as if about to charge, then both reared and clashed against each other in a growling, hissing frenzy of claws and fangs, rolling over and over, scrambling for dominance.

Amber lowered her camera for a moment, and Marco murmured, "She is testing him to be sure he is a worthy mate for her. But he is strong and virile. She will submit to him in the end."

Now the black beast was on top, snarling, and the female suddenly stilled, lying half on her side as he straddled her. Through her zoom lens Amber could see the faint markings of typical jaguar rosettes with centre spots in his glossy coat.

He licked the female's neck and she turned her head, lifting it to nuzzle at him, making a soft sound almost like a purr. Amber let out a quietly whispered, "Oh!"

The male's black head rested on the female's neck, his paws, claws retracted, kneaded her body. Despite the earlier tussle, her hide was unmarked.

The male adjusted their position, and the muscles in his powerful haunches began moving rhythmically.

Feeling like a voyeur, Amber was nevertheless caught in the magic of the moment, there seemed to be such anomalous tenderness in this savage mating.

The female's amber eyes almost closed. The male's movements stopped and he gave her what looked like a teasing, amorous bite on her shoulder before lifting himself away and trotting out of sight. For a while his mate remained where she was, then lazily rolled onto her back for a few seconds and repeated the movement several times, as if ecstatic, before stretching out, her side rising and falling with her breathing. She looked thoroughly content.

The black male reappeared, stared about suspiciously, his tail weaving the air. He appeared to home in on the two humans watching, his ears pricking up. Amber was almost certain he had seen them.

"Don't move," Marco breathed in her ear. He had the rifle in his hands.

It seemed an eternity before the jaguar turned his attention to his mate and padded over to her, lying down at her side, still watchful as if guarding her. It was getting dark now and his eyes were luminous, eerily glowing. Eventually he yawned, settled his big head between his paws and apparently slept.

"Come." Marco silently rose, and when he helped her up Amber realised her legs were stiff. She followed him as quietly as she could back to the cabin, still spellbound by what they'd been privileged to see.

Making love to her that night, Marco turned her over onto her stomach and she felt his strong body cover her, the gentle nip of his teeth on her shoulder even as he found the slick, yearning centre of her awaiting him, and he filled her over and over while she buried her screams of ecstasy in the pillow.

CHAPTER THIRTEEN

THE day following their return to the hacienda, Marco told Amber, "Next week I must go to Barinhas on business. We will take Madre and Ana Maria, and you can choose a wedding dress. Ana Maria knows all the best clothing stores."

"A wedding dress?"

"As the padre pointed out to me," he said rather dryly, "you were cheated of a proper wedding day. My mother too wants our marriage celebrated in the traditional manner. Perhaps your family would like to be here."

"I don't know if they can afford—"

"I will be happy to pay their fares, and they will of course stay here as guests of the family."

The dress was fabulous. Deceptively simple in style, but made sumptuous with shimmering satin and delicate lace.

She'd argued about using Marco's credit card, but had given in when he said, "It is part of our agreement. There is no need for you to make such an expense."

The reminder had stopped her cold. Sometimes she could almost—almost—forget that theirs was not a normal marriage, that love had played no part in its genesis.

Three weeks later she stood before the long, gilt-edged

mirror in Señora Salzano's room while the *señora,* Ana Maria and her own mother and sister fussed over her.

Ana Maria had taken charge of her make-up and styled her hair, crowned with a circlet of flowers.

"Are you sure about this, Amber?" Azure asked anxiously, when the others had left to check their own appearance. "Tell me truthfully, do you love him?"

Amber replied after the smallest hesitation. "Yes. Marco shouldn't have done what he did, but I don't think either of us understands completely how hard it was for him to let Benny go. He isn't mean or nasty, just…very focused on the things that are important to him."

"And not used to being thwarted," Azure added.

Sometimes she showed surprising insight. "True," Amber conceded. "But he has compromised hugely on this."

Amber had held her breath when her sister arrived with Rickie and their son. She'd seen how Marco had to tear his gaze away from the child sleeping against Rickie's shoulder, turning to greet her parents. And how later Azure had watched nervously when the little boy, losing his initial shyness, approached Marco and was lifted into his arms. Amber saw the fleeting tension in her husband's face.

When Benny reached up and patted his cheek, he'd smiled and then looked across at Azure, also watching him with anxious eyes. "I have two beautiful nieces," he said. "Thank you for giving me a nephew to love also."

And now he had met Benny, Amber thought, he wouldn't want to give up that link, would he? He'd said he would be an honorary godfather. He wanted to be involved, if peripherally, in Benny's life.

Even if he didn't love her, he'd want their marriage to last, legally at least.

Azure had looked as though she wanted to snatch her

child back, and Amber quickly crossed to her side, a smile on her mouth to hide from the others the warning in her eyes.

Gradually Azure had relaxed over the next few days. Now she gave Amber a hug and said, hopefully, "Well, if you're happy, I'm glad it turned out okay. I can't thank you enough for what you did. And you look beautiful!"

Turning to the mirror again, Amber saw that it was true. She hoped Marco would think so, that he would fall in love when he saw her, and never want to let her go.

The traditional solemn marriage rite in the little village church was far more emotive than the brief, cold ceremony back home that she'd never mentioned to her parents or sister. Making her vows in careful Spanish, and then in English for the benefit of her family, her voice trembled, and Marco's hand tightened on hers, his dark eyes burning, compelling.

The church was crowded; members of Marco's extended family, his *llaneros* and the families that farmed around the village all attended, spilling into the square outside.

Giving Amber a warm embrace on the church steps, Marco's mother said, "Now you are really married to my son, you must call me *Mamá* Salzano."

She had arranged a huge wedding feast at the hacienda.

There was dancing and singing to the sounds of Venezuelan harps, four-string guitars and maracas far into the night, and when Marco and Amber danced the *joropo* together, all of the guests erupted in thunderous applause, clapping in time to the music.

It began almost like a romantic waltz, the music slow as Marco held her close and then expertly swung her to his side, his head turned to hers and his lips only inches from her mouth. His strong hands guided her through a series of simple steps that she followed faultlessly, and the music quickened to a fast, foot-stamping crescendo. He never took his gaze from her face except to twirl her, always bringing her back into his arms. Marco gave her a dazzling smile as they whirled ever faster, his eyes alight with pleased surprise.

"How did you learn our national dance?" he asked as he held her in his arms after the final flourish. He kissed her quickly on the lips and waved to their audience.

"Ana Maria," she said breathlessly, "taught me. And I've watched the *llaneros* dancing it with their women."

He laughed. "What other secrets are you keeping from me, *mi esposa?*"

Amber shook her head. *I love you* was a secret too new and fragile to express. He had never asked for her love, never offered love to her. If he couldn't reciprocate her feelings he might find the confession an unwelcome burden.

But today they had been married in his church, and he too had made vows. If she gave him what he wanted so badly he might come to love her, even if only out of gratitude.

When they finally went to bed, as dawn broke over the vast flatlands, perhaps she imagined that Marco's lovemaking was extra tender, adoring her body almost as if this were their true consummation. As if he'd really meant it when he promised to love and cherish her until death.

The celebrations went on for three days before the guests began to leave. Elena had worn a wistful look as she gathered with the family at the church, and Amber had felt sympathy, but even Elena was swept into the dancing and partying, one young man particularly attentive.

Saying goodbye to her family at the end of their week-long stay, Amber was relieved that their lack of Spanish and Señora Salzano's limited English precluded any in-depth conversation about how she and Marco had met.

As the *hato* returned to normal, Amber realised that with the whirlwind preparations for the wedding and the excitement of seeing her family, she had lost track of her monthly cycle, which had never been reliably regular.

And maybe that was exactly why she'd missed a period. Stress—even the pleasant kind—could be a cause.

A test with the kit she kept in the bathroom was less than conclusive. The instructions said false negatives were more likely than false positives. She forced herself to wait another week.

This time there was no doubt.

It was Sunday morning and later they would be going to church, but she'd visited the bathroom early, when the sky was a pale, luminous pink. Marco was still in bed but awake, propped against the pillows with his hands behind his head, looking…enigmatic.

She said, "It looks as though I'm pregnant."

The words seemed to fall into a void between them. She wondered if he'd heard.

He lowered his arms with no discernible change of expression. "I have wondered when you were going to tell me."

Of course he'd have been keeping an eye on the calendar. This, after all, was why he'd married her. Try as she would to forget that, the reality every now and then hit her like a splash of icy water, bringing to the fore the persistent hidden ache she couldn't quite ignore.

Lately—ever since what she thought of as their "real" wedding day—when they made love, he had been extra gentle, sensitive to her every move, every murmur or sigh of pleasure, satisfying her fully while holding back himself. Not that passion was lacking, but she felt a subtle difference in his touch, his kisses. In and out of bed, he treated her like something precious and breakable. Last night she'd dared hope it meant his feelings were changing, becoming deeper. She'd gone to sleep in his arms bathed in a warm glow of cautious joy.

Had all that careful handling been not for her, but to protect the baby he had guessed she carried? She said, "I wanted to be sure of a positive test before saying anything."

"We will see a doctor to be certain, make sure everything is as it should be."

His voice was neutral, and she stood uncertainly in the middle of the room, feeling suddenly alone and frightened, all last night's warmth and wonder seeping away. The responsibility of having created—co-created—a new life, another human being, struck her as something so huge and powerful she wasn't ready for it.

"Are you all right?" Marco flung back the covers and strode to her.

She wanted him to take her in his strong arms, hold her close. Instead he stopped and lightly laid his hands on her shoulders, soothed the goose-flesh on her arms but otherwise didn't touch her.

"I'm fine," she said mechanically. Physically she didn't feel any different. Without knowing what she had expected of Marco, this calm acceptance somehow bothered her.

"I will make sure you are taken care of," he said. "You and our son."

Amber didn't doubt it. He would do anything necessary to ensure this baby was born safely, and that meant taking care of the woman who housed it. Her body, that he enjoyed so much, admired and caressed and played like a violin, bringing it into singing, extraordinary harmony with his, would become distorted and clumsy with the burden of his child. Unattractive.

She should remember that for him sexual pleasure was

a bonus, a nice perk. Basically she was no more than an incubator for Marco's longed-for child.

He said, "Is there anything you need? Anything I can get for you?"

Amber shrugged out of his hold. "All I need right now," she said, retreating to the bathroom, "is a shower."

So cool, Marco thought as Amber closed the door between them. Foolishly he had hoped, after the harmony of their brief "honeymoon," the solemn religious marriage ceremony and all they had shared since, that she would be happy to share this with him, to stay with him as his wife and the mother of their child.

A strange, black heaviness descended on him. There was no going back now. And more than ever the burden of guilt weighed on him, coupled with dread.

She is not Emilia, he told himself. Aurelio's birth was a freak event, Emilia was so small, almost delicate. This will be different. Yet fear laid an iron hand on his heart.

What madness had possessed him to think Amber would ever look forward to having his child? He had done this to her and now there was no going back.

May God forgive me. But it was not God's forgiveness he craved. And how could he dare even ask for Amber's?

The specialist Marco insisted on consulting said Amber needed a good, balanced diet and moderate exercise to keep healthy and prepare her body for labour. Marco vetoed horse-riding, and she was limited to walking and swimming, with gentle workouts on the home gym that Ana Maria religiously used. It was much less fun now Ana Maria had returned to university. "Mamá Salzano" was quietly pleased and joined her son in ensuring Amber had adequate food and rest, and did nothing that could harm the baby.

Amber began to feel like a prisoner.

Occasionally she persuaded Marco or Diego or even Elena to take her out in one of the all-terrain vehicles with her camera. With Diego she had updated and extended the Internet site, which now featured several clips of her work. She was also editing a feature and researching TV outlets for it.

But she'd explored only a small part of the vast estate, seen relatively few of its wild inhabitants.

The rains came, and came, and came—day after day, flattening the coarse grasses of the *llanos,* soaking the ground, flooding huge areas of the plains.

Marco regularly flew her to Barinhas for checkups, but after two ultrasounds, because of the baby's position in the womb, medics were unable to determine its sex.

"If they'd said it's a girl," she asked, flying home after the last test, "would you have wanted a termination?"

"An abortion?" His brows knotted fiercely. "Certainly not! You are not to think of such a thing."

Well, at least they were of the same mind on that. She would never have agreed.

The day Amber first felt the baby move, she was in the courtyard alone, tending the flowers in their pots, a duty she had taken over as something she could do without incurring Marco's displeasure.

She dropped the secateurs in her hand and put her palm to her abdomen, thinking maybe she was mistaken, but again she felt the movement, a fluttering of her tiny passenger, unmistakably something she'd never felt before.

Thinking Marco was working in his study with Elena,

she went inside and along the passageway, eager to share the news with him, and threw open the door without knocking, to find Elena standing alongside the filing cabinet, gazing at a framed picture in her hand.

When Amber entered, Elena quickly turned away, and the picture hit the corner of the open drawer, smashing the glass with a sharp sound. It dropped to the floor.

Elena seemed frozen in horror, and Amber quickly crossed to pick up the picture. "I'm sorry, Elena," she said. "I didn't mean to startle you."

She turned the frame, broken at one corner, to examine the damage and pick out the rest of the ruined glass, only then seeing the smiling woman and child in the photograph.

Elena snatched it from her, holding it to her chest. Her eyes were wide and her lips trembled.

"I'm so sorry," Amber reiterated. "The photo isn't damaged," she said gently. "We can get another frame. It's Emilia, isn't it? Marco's wife, and their son."

Elena nodded, still clutching the picture close. "It should be on the top of the cabinet, where he could see it from his desk. I found it at the back of the drawer." Her dark eyes flashed and her pretty mouth twisted bitterly. "All Emilia's pictures are gone, except in my own room. He tries to forget her now because he is *loco* for you."

I wish! Amber thought wryly. Had he placed the picture there so that he could secretly take it out and remind himself of his double loss? Remember when he and Emilia had been together with their little boy, a happy family?

Aloud she said, "He won't forget her, Elena." Her voice was husky with effort. "I know he loved her very much. He had her pictures put away to save my feelings. I don't suppose he realised how much it hurt you."

Disturbed by Elena's tragic, hostile stare, she crouched to pick up some glass.

"Amber?" Marco's voice made her jump, and a sliver of glass dug into her palm. "What are you doing?"

Amber hastily stood, and Elena, looking totally miserable, dumbly held out the picture for him to see.

He frowned. "You dropped it?"

Amber said quickly, drawing his attention, "Elena's not to blame. I am. I came in after she found it and I—"

He wasn't listening, taking one stride to catch her wrist and look at the blood welling on her hand. *"¡Ay, Dios mío!"* he exclaimed. "What have you done to yourself?"

"It's nothing—I was cleaning up the broken glass."

He said something explosive in Spanish and then, "We have staff to do that! Elena—call Filipa, tell her to bring the first aid kit." Grabbing the waste paper bin near the desk, he ordered Amber, "Put the glass in here."

"Shouldn't it be wrapped?" she objected, not wanting someone to cut themselves when disposing of the bin's contents. But at his hiss of impatience she complied. Blood was welling from the small wound at a surprising rate, and she didn't want it to fall on the beautiful woven rug.

She looked about for a box of tissues, but Marco had pulled a folded, unused white handkerchief from his pocket, and he pressed it against her palm.

When the maid brought in the first aid kit he took it from her and dressed Amber's hand himself, then told Filipa to sweep up the rest of the glass and dispose of it, and she hurried out of the room.

Elena stood by silently watching his ministrations, still holding the photograph, then suddenly burst into a torrent of Spanish too fast for Amber to follow, except for her own name and Emilia's, until Marco said something curt and harsh, and she ran from the room with the photo.

Amber said, "She's upset. I'm really sorry about the damage to the photo."

He looked at her closely. "Why did you do it?"

For a moment she gaped at him. "It was an accident!"

What had Elena said in that passionate outburst? Amber had been taught at an early age that telling tales was mean and ignoble, unless to prevent actual physical harm. The habit of a lifetime prevailed. "There's some misunderstanding," she said weakly.

Filipa arrived holding a short broom and a shovel and began sweeping up the rest of the glass, and Amber closed her lips, unwilling to continue the conversation in front of the maid, even though the woman evidently didn't understand a word of English.

"You admitted you were to blame," Marco said.

Amber shook her head. "I'd rather not discuss it now." Nor did she feel this was the time to tell him that she'd felt his baby move. That moment of euphoria and excitement had passed. "I have things to do before dinner," she said, and slipped past Filipa to return to the patio and the dead blooms she'd been snipping off.

At dinner a subdued Elena avoided Amber's anxious eyes, later slipping off early to her room. When Amber and Marco were alone later preparing for bed, she asked him, "What did Elena say this afternoon before she rushed off?"

"Quite a lot," he said. "But it need not concern you."

"Neither of us meant to damage the photograph." Amber briefly told him what had happened.

He merely nodded, his expression not giving anything away. When she added, "I think Elena was distressed that you'd taken her cousin's picture from its place. Would it disturb you if it were repaired and put back there?"

Marco's short laugh was oddly harsh. "Is that what you would like me to do?"

"For Elena's sake, yes." Perhaps for his too she thought, suppressing the pang that gave her. "I appreciate you were trying to save my feelings, but I can't ignore or forget that you were married to someone else and had a child with her. It's been the elephant in the room ever since I came here."

"Elephant?" Marco shook his head, his brows rising.

"The thing that everyone pretends isn't there," she explained. "Even though it's so big you can't miss it."

"Ah," he said, enlightenment in his face. After a brief pause he said, with a strangely resigned expression, "Very well. I will tell Elena to get a new frame and return the picture to its accustomed place." Under his breath he muttered something else, but she caught only the word *penitencia*. Penance? She didn't dare ask.

Within a few days the photo reappeared on top of the filing cabinet, in a new frame. Amber didn't ask where that had come from—perhaps Elena had removed another picture from it. She seemed to mellow towards Amber from then on, and one day when they were alone she said abruptly, "I'm sorry for those things I said to Marco about you. You are not what I thought. He told me you asked him to put Emilia's picture back."

"I have no idea what you thought. Or said to Marco."

Elena flushed. "That you were a…a gold digger, I think is the English term. That you had hypnotised him with sex, made him forget the sweetest, prettiest, most loving wife any man could have, who adored him."

Almost exactly the same words that Marco had used to describe Emilia.

"He won't forget your cousin," Amber said, thinking how ironically far off the mark Elena's view was. "Nor Aurelio. He can't, and I wouldn't want him to. Only…I would like him to be happy."

Elena gave her a strange look. "I, too, would like that for Marco," she said. "Are *you* happy, Amber?"

"Of course." *Was* she? Certainly closer to it than she had expected before leaving her homeland. She and Marco had sex less often lately, but he was solicitous when she had bouts of nausea or was simply tired. When they did make love he was cautious, afraid of hurting her or the baby despite the doctor's assurance there should be no problem. Every night he slept at her side, and as the months went on he spent more time at the hacienda. Yet somehow he seemed emotionally to be growing more distant.

Amber remembered wistfully their closeness at the *campamento*, when he'd even allowed her to comfort him over the loss of his son and his wife. All that seemed to have disappeared under a mask of courtesy and care that held little real warmth.

He was pleased that she had developed a growing appreciation of his country, its language, customs and turbulent history. Once he took her to Caracas for several days, where they attended concerts and exhibitions, and she absorbed the rich cultural life of the city with its diverse population and the constant throb and strum of music combining Spanish and African, indigenous Indian and modern American themes and rhythms.

At last she went into labour and was taken to the hospital to give birth. The following hours were a blur of pain and effort, with doctors and nurses giving encouragement and efficiently guiding the process. Marco held her hand in a hard, warm grip while he stroked her hair or wiped her forehead with a cool cloth and talked in a calm, reassuring voice, telling her she was brave, beautiful, magnificent, in English and in Spanish.

Then it was all over and she felt a surge of relief and euphoria like nothing she'd every experienced before.

A tiny bundle of warmth was placed on her breast and she looked into fathomless dark eyes that blinked sleepily from a round little face with a rosebud mouth, and scarcely heard the voice of one of the medical staff say, "Congratulations, *señora*. You have a beautiful baby girl!"

She must have slept for hours. When she woke a nurse was lifting the wailing baby from a bassinet beside the bed, depositing it into Amber's arms as soon as she'd managed to sit up. The nurse helped her bare her swollen breasts and beamed with satisfaction as the baby nuzzled about and found its target, settling comfortably to suckling.

Amber would never forget that moment, when absolute love and awe filled her, gazing down at the oblivious little face with its curved cheek and minuscule nose and cap of wavy dark hair, while unbelievably small, fragile fingers clutched at her skin.

After the nurse left, Marco entered, carrying a huge bouquet and looking big and handsome and turning Amber's heart over just at the sight of him.

She admired the flowers and he put them on the cabinet at her side before pulling over the visitor's chair and seating himself. "How do you feel?" he asked Amber.

"Wonderful," she answered, glancing up at him. Oddly shy, she went back to gazing at the baby.

"Your parents are on their way," he said, making her raise her eyes to him in surprise. "I thought you would like to have them with you."

"That's thoughtful of you," she said. "They'll be thrilled with their new grandchild." She guessed that he had insisted on paying the fares. "You're very generous, Marco. I'm grateful."

He too seemed somehow uncomfortable, even stressed, his eyes deeper in their sockets, the skin stretched over the bones of his face. "You have no cause to be grateful to me, Amber," he said. "I am sorry for what I have put you through."

The guilt of a new father after watching a woman deliver his child in blood, sweat and tears. Some women in labour, she'd been told, cursed the man who had made them pregnant. She'd simply been grateful that he was there with his calm, steady support; although, she had seen the sheen of sweat on his brow that matched hers, seen the tautness of his jaw suggesting an inner tension.

All she felt now was a serenity like no other. Only one faint shadow remained. Unable to imagine that Marco didn't share her feelings for this tiny scrap of humanity that they had created, that he had helped her coax and push into the world, she said, "I know you wanted a boy, but maybe next time…"

"Next time…?" He got up suddenly, pushing back his chair so hard that it started to topple and he grabbed it and put it upright. "*You* can say that?"

The baby abruptly stopped suckling and wriggled inside her covering, making little snuffling noises. Amber lifted the infant against her shoulder, closing the gown over her breasts. A cold sense of foreboding crept up on her. Recalling what Marco had said about his first wife—that after her difficult childbirth he wouldn't subject her to another—she said, "I'm strong and healthy. There's no reason I can't have another baby, in time."

"I hope you do," Marco said in a strangely muffled tone, "but not mine."

The chill increased, and her voice sounded thready when she said, "What do you mean?"

He wasn't looking at her, instead staring at the floor, hands thrust into his pockets. She saw his knuckles through the fabric as if he'd clenched his fists. "I have booked a flight for you and your baby to fly to New Zealand with your parents, in ten days' time. A one-way ticket."

Shock made her dizzy and speechless. Her limbs seemingly made of lead, she turned and placed the baby back into the bassinet, tucking in the covers as if the trivial action were the most important task in the world.

Her heart was leaden too, beating slowly, suffocatingly. "*My* baby?" she repeated.

"Of course I will pay for her upbringing, her education—anything she needs," Marco said, his tone colourless. "Or that you need." He might have been discussing the care of his cattle. "Apart from that…I'm sure you will give her a good upbringing."

Amber's heart was splintering into a thousand pieces. At the same time anger began to simmer, breaking through the paralysing cold and fear that gripped her.

Marco had counted on a boy, and because she'd given him a girl he was cutting his losses, denying the baby the right to know her father, hurling Amber's unspoken love back in her face. Sending them away because she'd failed in the one thing he'd wanted from her, the one thing he'd married her for, that she'd almost lost sight of because she'd foolishly, *idiotically* fallen in love with him.

Fallen in love, forgetting how cold-bloodedly he'd engineered their marriage, how ruthlessly he'd exploited her love for her family, her fear for the future of her sister's baby, forgetting the very basis of her relationship with him—that if she didn't meet the conditions he'd laid down he'd dispense with her. As he was dispensing with the child he didn't want.

"You *bastard!*" she spat. "You heartless, selfish, sexist barbarian!"

She should have seen the signs—they'd been there. The practised seduction, the efforts to resign her to her fate with cunning and patience, his encouragement of her filming, the magical "honeymoon" at the *campamento,* enchanting her with its wildlife and putting his own spell on her with his lovemaking.

And then, after she was pregnant, a gradual withdrawal, an aloofness she was unable to penetrate. Because he thought he'd achieved his goal, and all he had to do now was wait until his child—his *son*—was safely born.

Even today he hadn't even glanced again at the baby. Not once. How could she have thought she loved this calculating, manipulative, unfeeling man?

Marco's jaw set tight. "I said I would let you go."

"When I gave you a son!"

He shrugged, with a seeming effort. "It makes no difference. I have arranged for your parents to stay at a hotel near here. It is best if I don't see you again." Something happened to his voice then, a sort of cracking. "Thank you, Amber, for our time together. I apologise from the bottom of my heart for what I did to you. It is impossible to make it right. I have been all you say—selfish, arrogant, a barbarian. I can only try my best to make it up to you."

He turned and opened the door, even as she tried to absorb that, make sense of it. "Marco?" she said to his implacable back.

He ignored her, stepping into the corridor.

She shoved back the bedcovers and somehow got hurriedly to her feet. *"Marco?"*

He might have been deaf.

"Marco!" Reaching the doorway, she held onto it because she was dizzy. Dimly she could see him rapidly walking away from her, skirting a couple in front of him, nodding to a passing nurse.

With an effort she stepped out into the corridor, screaming at him with all the energy and fury she could muster, "*Marco Salzano,* don't you *dare* walk out on me—on your daughter!" She tried to say more, but her lips wouldn't work and the corridor was turning darker. Then, even though her eyes were open, she saw only blackness and finally nothing at all.

Leaving the room, Marco resolutely kept his eyes focused straight ahead. He was doing the right thing—far too late, but he had to go through with this. Had to, however inadequately, give back to Amber whatever he could of her own life. And sacrifice his baby, his and Amber's beautiful baby girl. No matter that it hurt so much he was afraid to look at her.

Taking long, rapid strides, he passed a couple in the corridor, stifling an urge to shove them out of his way, so black was his mood.

He had always known that a child would bind Amber to him. But he also knew that he wanted more from her than a reluctant commitment, more than her lifelong bondage for the sake of her child. More, much more, than her sexual surrender and the delights of her body.

He wanted her love. Even though he'd tried to blind himself to his own need at first, *that* was the real, underlying reason he had been unable to fly home and leave her in New Zealand.

And how could a woman like her love a man who had descended to such depths to win her? She could feel nothing but hatred for such a man.

The nurse he automatically nodded to as he strode away from any chance of happiness gave him a startled look. He realised he appeared the antithesis of a delighted new father, with a scowl on his brow and his eyes bleak with steely determination—and grief.

His guilt had increased daily with the progress of Amber's pregnancy, peaked as she struggled in agony to deliver his child.

Now her voice, sounding both desperate and angry as she called his name, challenged his cowardly retreat, made him wince. He gritted his teeth and kept walking.

He heard a muffled thud, an exclamation, and turned to see the nurse hurrying towards a crumpled form outside the door of one of the rooms.

Amber.

Without thought he was running back, passing the nurse halfway and dropping to his knees beside the still, ashen-faced body, choking out her name.

The nurse arrived beside him, checked Amber's pulse, asked, "She's your wife, *señor?*"

"Yes." Marco said. "My wife." *My wife, to have and to hold...* But he must not think that.

Deathly afraid, he obeyed the nurse's brisk request to carry the patient back to her room.

Gently he lowered Amber to the bed, relieved to see her eyelids flutter and consciousness return as she focused dazed green eyes on him.

"Marco," she said. Her hand moved, apparently aim-lessly, and he caught it in his, smoothing back her tumbled hair from her cold forehead with the other. She seemed to be comforted by that, her eyes closing, a hint of colour returning to her cheeks.

He held his breath, thinking his heart was going to burst with fear and love. It had been the same while she was having the baby, her lovely face contorted with effort, sweating, gasping, grunting—praying. He had never felt so helpless in his life, nor so guilt-stricken, not even after Emilia and Aurelio died, when in the depths of despair he'd blamed himself for not being able to save them.

Nor when he'd brought Amber to the home that held their ghosts, unable to shake the feeling that he was betraying their memory by wanting another woman with a desire so fierce and relentless that he'd forced her into an insane bargain. Not able to even face their photographs, pretending to himself as well as his mother that it was Amber's feelings he was sparing.

Amber, who hadn't cared anyway. Who, far from being upset by reminders of a previous love, had urged him to restore Emilia and Aurelio's portrait to its place.

While he had squirmed with an irrational jealousy of her easy friendship with Diego, she had not felt even a twinge of that emotion.

Because she did not—could not—love him. This too was his fault—the pallor of her skin, her bloodless lips, the coldness of her hands, the glazed look in her eyes.

It had taken all his willpower to walk away from her, set her free to live her life without him. But with the daughter he had loved from the first moment he'd seen the wet, bloody, slippery little tadpole that she was at birth. He'd been afraid to look at her as she lay on her mother's breast taking her first breaths. He'd known right then, with the piercing pain of imminent loss, that he had no right to hold either of them, neither her nor her mother.

A doctor hurried into the room after the nurse and Marco allowed them space to take her blood pressure, check Amber's pulse again, ask questions that Amber weakly answered. Finally they left, saying, "You fainted, is all. Don't get out of bed too quickly. We'll leave you with your husband." And to him in Spanish, "Ring the bell if you are worried."

Marco stared down at his sleeping daughter. He lifted his gaze to Amber and saw her eyes widen, knew she had seen his suffering. "Thank you," she said, "for coming back."

He shut his eyes tightly, turned away to swipe with an impatient hand across the hot stinging of his eyes and, making himself face her, said in a guttural voice, "Do not thank me, Amber. It is what you call coals to Newcastle."

For a moment she looked blank, then to his surprise she emitted a shaky, girlish giggle. "You mean coals of fire, I think. It wasn't your fault I fainted."

"You are wrong. Everything that has happened since we met is my fault. I have sinned against God and against you. Against my own…morals, principles. I told myself I was entitled, that because you had conspired with your sister to hide her son from me it was not criminal to force you to be my wife. But the truth was, I wanted *you*. You. And a baby—your baby—to hold you to me."

"But—"

"I will keep my promise to let you go," he ground out, against every instinct, "but—" momentarily he closed his eyes again, composing himself "—*why* did you call me back? You have made it doubly hard."

Amber had seen the anguish in his eyes. *"Why?"* she asked, afraid to believe in the hope that stirred inside her. "Why is it so hard?"

He opened his eyes, and they blazed. "Because I cannot live without you—no, I must. I will not ask you to forgive me for the unforgivable. This is the penance I deserve. It is for your sake, and for hers." His gaze flickered to the crib, and then he seemed unable to drag his eyes away. "A part of you—and a part of me also. At least that knowledge you cannot take from me."

Amber blinked. "I don't want to take anything away from you, Marco!" What was he saying? "You kept insisting on a son, but…you *want* her? You think you could love her?"

He groaned, actually groaned aloud. "Of course I want her!" he growled, and drew a harsh breath. "I have loved her from the moment I first saw her. Almost as much as I love you."

Amber stared, momentarily unable to speak. "Me?"

"*Madre de Dios!* How can you not know? I have loved you since—I think since I first knew you were not your sister. You were so fierce to protect your family, so determined to defy me, even though I knew that in another time, another place, we might have been lovers. I *had* to have you, keep you at my side. I was *loco*—arrogant and *estúpido* enough to think I could make you love me."

Amber felt hope slowly becoming certainty, then a starburst of revelation.

Marco loved her. Hadn't she seen it in everything he'd done since taking her to his home—in every gesture, every touch, every look? In his patience and determined gentleness, his care of her even when she repudiated it, impatient with his over-protectiveness.

She swallowed, found her voice. "What you did was monstrous—" she saw him wince at that "—and if you ever pull a stunt like that again, I'll…I'll…haul you over those red-hot coals from Newcastle," she finished lamely. "It's what you deserve. But—" she looked at the baby, obliviously sleeping at her side "—you gave me the best gift of my whole life. For her sake alone I'd forgive you, if I wasn't already in love with you."

Marco shook his head. "In love with me?" He seemed dazed.

"*Yes!* And if you send me away I'll come back to Hato El Paraíso and camp on your doorstep, in a tent if I have to. With our baby. You wouldn't do *that* to your daughter, would you?"

Marco sank heavily on the bed, taking both her hands in his. "No, *querida.* Never." Regaining some of his usual manner, he said, "I will not have it! But you must be sure this is what you want, because I may never let you go. Oh, holidays, *sí.* For a little while, to see your family. Not to leave me, to tear my heart apart."

"I couldn't," Amber said simply. "And besides, I won't deprive our baby of a father. She needs you, almost as much as I do."

"As I need you, *mi corazón,*" he said fervently. *My heart.*

She'd never thought Marco could sound so humble. It was almost scary that she could do this to him, a man who had never shown vulnerability before.

Then he leaned over and kissed her, and she held him close with her arms about him, goading him from gentleness to passion until he wrenched himself away, saying, "Enough! You are not fit yet for this." He stood, drawing in deep breaths, his hands clutching the rim of the bassinet. "Have you given her a name?" he asked.

"No. Do you have any preference?"

Marco shook his head. Then he said, "*Sí.* Generosa. In honour of her mother. Its meaning is *generous.*"

Amber tried the name. "Generosa." She looked at the baby. "Genny for short? Or Rosa. She looks like a rose."

As if she had heard, the baby stirred, opened her eyes, screwed up her face and sneezed. Both her parents laughed, enchanted at what they had made between them. Marco leaned down and whispered, "Generosa?"

She stared up at him, gave a contented little grunt and closed her eyes again.

Marco leaned down and kissed her forehead. "Generosa," he said. "I think she approves."

"Yes." Amber held out her hand to him, and he took it again in his, raising it to his lips.

"You must rest," he ordered sternly, tucking her hand under the covers.

For once Amber would be happy to obey. When she was not so tired she would teach him to be less autocratic, for their daughter's sake. Already she imagined a teenager with Marco's black hair and strong will, dark eyes flashing at his protective restrictions. She smiled. "You can go now," she said. "I suppose you have things to take care of."

"No. Only you," he assured her. "I am yours," he promised, "for as long as you want me."

"I want you. Always." She closed her eyes, serene in the knowledge that he was watching over her and their child, that whatever predators or demons he had to fight, from outside or within himself, her very own conquistador would keep them safe for the rest of their lives.

* * * * *

*Turn the page for an exclusive extract
from Harlequin Presents®*

THE PLAYBOY SHEIKH'S VIRGIN STABLE-GIRL
by
Sharon Kendrick

Claimed by the sheikh—for her innocence!

Polo-playing Sheikh Prince Kaliq Al'Farisi loves his
women as much as his horses. They're wild, willing
and he's their master!

Stable girl Eleni is a local Calistan girl. Raised by her
brutal father on the horse racing circuit, she feels
unlovable. When her precious horses are given to
Sheikh Kaliq she *refuses* to be parted from them.

The playboy sheikh is determined to bed her, and
when he realizes she's a virgin the challenge only
becomes more interesting. However, Kaliq is torn; his
body wants Eleni, yet his heart wants to protect her….

"WHAT WOULD YOU SAY, MY DAUGHTER, if I told you that a royal prince was coming to the home of your father?"

She would say that he *had* been drinking, after all. But never to his face, of course. If Papa was having one of his frequent flights of fancy then it was always best to play along with it.

Eleni kept her face poker-straight. "A royal prince, Papa?" she questioned gravely.

"Yes, indeed!" He pushed his face forward. "The Prince Kaliq Al'Farisi," he crowed, "is coming to my house to play cards with me!"

Her father had gone insane! These were ideas of grandeur run riot! And what was Eleni to do? What if he continued to make such idle boasts in front of the men who were sitting waiting to begin the long night of card-playing? Surely that would make him a laughingstock and ruin what little reputation he had left.

"Papa," she whispered urgently, "I beg you to think clearly. What place would a royal prince have *here?*"

But she was destined never to hear a reply, even though his mouth had opened like a puppet's, for there came the sound of distant hooves. The steady, powerful thud of horses as they thundered over the parched sands. On the still, thick air the muffled beat grew closer and louder until it filled Eleni's ears like the sound of the desert wolves that howled at the silver moon when it was at its fullest.

Toward them galloped a clutch of four horses, and as Eleni watched, one of them broke free and surged forward like a black stream of oil gushing out of the arid sand. For a moment, she stood there, transfixed—for this was as beautiful and as reckless a piece of riding as she had ever witnessed.

Illuminated by the orange-gold of the dying sun, she saw a colossus of a man with an ebony stallion between his thighs that he urged on with a joyful shout. The man's bare head was as dark as the horse he rode and his skin gleamed like some bright and burnished metal. Robes of pure silk clung to the hard sinews of his body. As he approached, Eleni could see a face so forbidding that some deep-rooted fear made her wonder if he had the power to turn to dust all those who stood before him.

And a face so inherently beautiful that it was as if all the desert flowers had bloomed at once.

It was then that Eleni understood the full and daunting truth. Her father's bragging *had* been true, and riding toward their humble abode was indeed Prince Kaliq Al'Farisi. Kaliq the daredevil, the lover of women, the playboy, the gambler and irresponsible twin son of Prince Ashraf. The man it was said could make women moan with pleasure simply by looking at them.

She had not seen him since she was a young girl in the crowds watching the royal family pass by. Back then, he had been doing his military service and wearing the uniform of the Calistan Navy. And back then he had been an arresting young man, barely out of his twenties. But now—a decade and a half on—he was at the most magnificent peak of his manhood, with a raw and beautiful masculinity that seemed to shimmer from his muscular frame.

"By the wolves that howl!" Eleni whimpered, and ran inside the house.

* * * * *

Be sure to look for
THE PLAYBOY SHEIKH'S VIRGIN STABLE-GIRL
by Sharon Kendrick,
available August 2009 from Harlequin Presents®!

HARLEQUIN *Presents*

TWO CROWNS, TWO ISLANDS, ONE LEGACY

*A royal family torn apart by pride and lust for power,
reunited by purity and passion*

THE ROYAL HOUSE of KAREDES

Pick up the next adventure in this passionate series!

THE PLAYBOY SHEIKH'S VIRGIN STABLE-GIRL
by Sharon Kendrick, August 2009

THE PRINCE'S CAPTIVE WIFE
by Marion Lennox, September 2009

THE SHEIKH'S FORBIDDEN VIRGIN
by Kate Hewitt, October 2009

THE GREEK BILLIONAIRE'S INNOCENT PRINCESS
by Chantelle Shaw, November 2009

THE FUTURE KING'S LOVE-CHILD
by Melanie Milburne, December 2009

RUTHLESS BOSS, ROYAL MISTRESS
by Natalie Anderson, January 2010

THE DESERT KING'S HOUSEKEEPER BRIDE
by Carol Marinelli, February 2010

Eight volumes to collect and treasure!

ROYAL AND RUTHLESS

Royally bedded, regally wedded!

A Mediterranean majesty, a Greek prince, a desert king and a fierce nobleman—with any of these men around, a royal bedding is imminent!

And when they're done in the bedroom, the next thing to arrange is a very regal wedding!

Look for all of these fabulous stories available in August 2009!

Innocent Mistress, Royal Wife #65
by ROBYN DONALD

The Ruthless Greek's Virgin Princess #66
by TRISH MOREY

The Desert King's Bejewelled Bride #67
by SABRINA PHILIPS

Veretti's Dark Vengeance #68
by LUCY GORDON

HARLEQUIN *Presents*

International Billionaires

*Life is a game of power and pleasure.
And these men play to win!*

BLACKMAILED INTO THE GREEK TYCOON'S BED
by *Carol Marinelli*

When ruthless billionaire Xante Rossi catches
mousy Karin red-handed, he designs a way to save
her from scandal. But she'll have to earn
the favor—in his bedroom!

Book #2846

Available August 2009

Look for the last installment of
International Billionaires from Harlequin Presents!

THE VIRGIN SECRETARY'S
IMPOSSIBLE BOSS
by *Carole Mortimer*
September 2009

www.eHarlequin.com   HP12846

REQUEST YOUR FREE BOOKS!

2 FREE NOVELS
PLUS 2
FREE GIFTS!

YES! Please send me 2 FREE Harlequin Presents® novels and my 2 FREE gifts (gifts are worth about $10). After receiving them, if I don't wish to receive any more books, I can return the shipping statement marked "cancel". If I don't cancel, I will receive 6 brand-new novels every month and be billed just $4.05 per book in the U.S. or $4.74 per book in Canada. That's a savings of close to 15% off the cover price! It's quite a bargain! Shipping and handling is just 50¢ per book*. I understand that accepting the 2 free books and gifts places me under no obligation to buy anything. I can always return a shipment and cancel at any time. Even if I never buy another book, the two free books and gifts are mine to keep forever.

106 HDN EYRQ   306 HDN EYR2

Name	(PLEASE PRINT)	
Address		Apt. #
City	State/Prov.	Zip/Postal Code

Signature (if under 18, a parent or guardian must sign)

Mail to the **Harlequin Reader Service:**
IN U.S.A.: P.O. Box 1867, Buffalo, NY 14240-1867
IN CANADA: P.O. Box 609, Fort Erie, Ontario L2A 5X3

Not valid to current subscribers of Harlequin Presents books.

Are you a current subscriber of Harlequin Presents books and want to receive the larger-print edition? Call 1-800-873-8635 today!

* Terms and prices subject to change without notice. Prices do not include applicable taxes. Sales tax applicable in N.Y. Canadian residents will be charged applicable provincial taxes and GST. Offer not valid in Quebec. This offer is limited to one order per household. All orders subject to approval. Credit or debit balances in a customer's account(s) may be offset by any other outstanding balance owed by or to the customer. Please allow 4 to 6 weeks for delivery. Offer available while quantities last.

Your Privacy: Harlequin Books is committed to protecting your privacy. Our Privacy Policy is available online at www.eHarlequin.com or upon request from the Reader Service. From time to time we make our lists of customers available to reputable third parties who may have a product or service of interest to you. If you would prefer we not share your name and address, please check here.

HP09R

You're invited to join Tell Harlequin Reader Panel

By joining our new reader panel you will:

- Receive Harlequin® books—they are FREE and yours to keep with no obligation to purchase anything!
- Participate in fun online surveys
- Exchange opinions and ideas with women just like you
- Have a say in our new book ideas and help us publish the best in women's fiction

In addition, you will have a chance to win great prizes and receive special gifts! See Web site for details. Some conditions apply. Space is limited.

To join, visit us at
www.TellHarlequin.com.

I ♥

HARLEQUIN *Presents*

BROUGHT TO YOU BY FANS OF
HARLEQUIN PRESENTS.

We are its editors and authors
and biggest fans—and we'd
love to hear from YOU!

Subscribe today to our online blog at
www.iheartpresents.com